HOCKEY HOUSE V-CARDS

A COLLEGE SPORTS ROMANCE

NOLAN U HOCKEY #0.5

KATY ARCHER

ISBN: 978-1-991138-00-2 (Kindle)
ISBN: 978-1-991138-33-0 (Paperback)

Archer Street Romance
www.katyarcher.com

ETHAN

THE SEX GOD

CHAPTER 1

I've been called a lot of things in my time.

Trouble.

Mischief.

Asshole.

Hottie.

Douche nugget.

Stud.

Sex god—that was a good one.

"Ethan!"

I pivot left, collecting the puck Casey just fired at me and screaming around the back of the goal. My skates cut into the ice as I round the end of the rink and flick my wrist, firing the puck into the net.

Even though there's no goalie in there right now...

Even though I've done that move a million times before...

It's always so fucking satisfying.

I glide around the cones laid out for practice and continue the drill, collecting pucks from various players and then passing them on to others or flicking them into the net.

The thwack of sticks hitting pucks and the swoosh of skates through the ice is my favorite kind of music, and I drown myself in it, needing the distraction more than anything.

I need this sweat, these aching muscles.

I have to be forced to concentrate on exactly what I'm doing in this moment, because if I don't... I'll think about her.

And if I think about her, it'll be a fresh kind of torture, because holy fuck... she was something else.

My lips twitch, and in spite of my resolve to put her from my mind, she skips right through it, her sassy little mouth calling me "Captain Hero" before she rolled her eyes and sarcastically quipped, "What do you want, a parade?"

I've never had a girl speak to me like that before. They usually melt and swoon, or give me their sexy eyes, trying to win me over, but this one didn't give two shits.

She just—

"Oof!" My shoulder smacks against the boards.

I grunt, shoving Jason off me as he laughs and skates backward. "Concentrate, dickweed!"

Dickweed. Another name to add to the list.

I extend my middle finger, pleased that my padded gloves don't hide the gesture. Jason growls and looks ready to whip off his gloves and come at me, but Coach shouts for his attention before he can.

Like I'd let that douchebag touch me.

I still can't believe he's the team captain. I mean, what the actual fuck?

I refuse to accept that Coach wasn't pressured into it by Jason's family somehow. That has got to be the only explanation. Those rich pricks have a way of getting what they want every fucking time, and it drives us all crazy.

Coach has got to be pissed that his hand's been forced. He's too professional to admit it, but I saw the set of his jaw when he made the announcement, and then he looked right at me, his hard gaze telling me what I needed to hear.

"I wanted it to be you."

It was a cold comfort, but I guess I'll have to take it. Jason will be graduating at the end of this year—thank fuck—and then I can step into the role that was supposed to be mine.

"You good, man?" Ice sprays up from Liam's skates as he jerks to a quick stop beside me.

"Yeah. Just Jason being Jason."

"He's such a cockwaffle."

My short snicker turns into a laugh before I can stop it. *Cockwaffle. Good one.*

I nudge my best friend with my elbow, and we skate back to the center of the rink. Liam flicks a puck my way, and I send it flying across the ice. Asher gathers it up, spinning around Casey and gliding it into the goal with a finesse that pisses me off.

Not because Asher's not awesome on the ice.

I want him doing exactly that kind of shit come game time.

I guess I'm still dark at him over what went down last night.

And that feeling only gets blacker when that short brunette starts skipping through my mind again, like a teasing little temptress.

One I can't have.

Thanks to Asher.

With a growl, I send another puck rocketing across the ice.

CHAPTER 2

I take longer in the shower than normal. I'm not sure why. Maybe I'm just delaying the inevitable.

It's Friday night after an intense practice. The best way to blow off steam is to hit up the local sports bar—Offside. It'll be packed full of testosterone and hotties. A horny hive of steamy looks and suggestive comments.

Girls will be shaking their booties on the dance floor, the hints of fabric barely covering their bodies enough to make a guy's brain stop working. Every cell in our stupid-ass heads will misfire, shooting all the blood down our bodies until the only thing left to do is act—make out, get down and dirty.

And I can't fucking do it.

Not tonight.

Not any night for another... shit, I don't even want to count it.

Turning off the shower with a growl, I ignore the

looks I'm getting, turning my back on my teammates and stalking into the locker room. They're not morons. They know exactly what my problem is.

Someone snickers behind me, and my shoulders tense. I will not turn around. They won't get the fucking satisfaction.

So I lost a bet.

So I acted like a cocky asshole.

And now I have to pay the price.

Like I'm going to let them know how much this is killing me.

No sex for a month is doable. I'm not some weak, pathetic loser.

But shit, I can't even jack off. Why the fuck did I shake on something so stupid?

Asher goaded me right into a corner, and I fell for it. Because the thought of that guy besting me was acid in my mouth.

I wanted to prove that I was the better man, and fuck me, I couldn't do it.

Wrestling my shirt down over slightly damp skin, I keep my back turned. I probably deserve the mockery. Shit, if I was on the other side of this thing, I'd probably be laughing too.

What kind of moron agrees to a sex-less month over a fucking game of darts?

Slamming my locker shut, I spin and eye up the room. They all jerk as if they haven't been staring at me, trying to look busy while we pack up and get ready to leave the stadium.

"Who's up for Offside?" Casey struts into the room butt naked from his shower. Water droplets are still dripping down his torso as he raises his thick arms in the air and shouts, "Time to get some booty, boys!"

A cheer rises around me. Even Jason is grinning and whooping.

And that's me out.

If he's gonna be there, I'm gonna not.

I can stomach the guy on a good day. But there's no fucking way I can handle him tonight.

"Hey." Liam taps my arm with the back of his hand. "Thought I might head back to Hockey House. Chill there tonight. You in?"

I narrow my eyes at him and shake my head. "You don't have to do that for me, man."

He shrugs. "Don't know what you're talking about. I *want* to go back to the house. Not really in the mood for Offside tonight."

"Yeah, right," I mutter but can't help a small smile.

This is why the guy's my best friend.

"Padre, you in?" Asher bounces over, gripping my buddy's shoulders.

I can't even remember where Liam picked up the nickname, but it must have been since college, because I never heard it in high school. It's fitting, I guess. The guy's like the papa bear of the house, always looking out for us.

"Nah, Ethan and I are just gonna chill at the house tonight."

Asher sticks out his lip in a girlish pout. "Aw. Can Ethan not handle the hotties? I wonder why that is."

I resist the urge to growl and smash my fist into his face. Keeping my expression neutral is a test of my control, especially when Asher starts laughing.

"Dude. Thirty more days. Yee-ouch!"

Clenching my jaw, I force a smile that is so fucking tight it can barely move my lips.

It just makes Asher laugh that much harder as he spins and heads off with the guys.

I sigh, dipping my chin while Liam slaps me on the shoulder. "It'll be over before you know it, man. You can do this."

I nod, shuffling after him as we leave the arena and head back to Hockey House.

The six-bedroom home is only a ten-minute drive from the hockey stadium. It's a sweet location and I'm grateful for it, even if it does mean I have to live with Asher. Thankfully, Liam, Casey, and Baxter live here, too, plus we get the rest of the team coming and going like they own the place. It helps ease the tension between Asher and me.

Look, the guy's not all bad.

He hooked us up with this place. He's a nice enough person, but he knows how to rub me up the wrong way, and I would have paid good money to lose this bet to anyone but him.

The house is empty when we get there. I dump my bag on the floor and slump into a chair. Liam goes into the kitchen, and I listen to him doing his thing. Cupboards open and shut, the microwave beeps and hums, something clatters, and five minutes later he's walking to the dining room table with two steaming bowls of ramen noodles and a bag of chips tucked under his arm.

"Thanks, man." I take my bowl and fork, shuffling in my seat and chowing down.

We eat in silence, which isn't unusual, I guess. But tonight it feels thick and awkward, and I get antsy pretty fast.

Liam, of course, notices. "Need to talk about it?"

"Nope."

"Liar." He snickers.

"What the fuck is there to say?"

"Yeah." He sighs. "I know it sucks. But it's only a month, right?"

I nod, stabbing my fork into the noodles and giving it a twist. Liam doesn't know about that girl I met last night. The one who wouldn't tell me her name. The one who keeps skipping through my brain like a siren. Shit, it's the worst timing possible.

She's a student on campus. I'm bound to bump into her again, right?

As hard as I try, I won't be able to stop looking for her, and then—

The front door clicks and swings open.

Liam and I both glance at the archway, waiting to see who'll appear.

Shit. It's Asher.

He swans in with a smile while my shoulders slump. I look at the tabletop, clenching my jaw and willing myself to calm the fuck down.

"Gentlemen." He sniffs, his nose wrinkling as he eyes up the noodles.

The guy's a food snob.

He tries to act like he isn't, but he can never hide it. He grew up with a silver spoon in his mouth, and it fucking shows.

"What are you doing here?" Liam asks, his tone mild. "Thought you were getting some at the bar tonight?"

Dumping a six-pack on the table, he subtly slides the bottles my way and looks between us. "Thought I'd bring the party to you. Not sure I could stand another second of Jackass Jason going on about what hot shit he is." He runs a hand through his dark hair, then rearranges it like he always does. "There's confident. There's cocky. And then there's just plain schmeef, you know?"

"Such a donkey boy," I mutter, shaking my head.

"That he is." Asher laughs, slapping me lightly on the shoulder before pulling out a beer and uncapping it for me.

He holds it out, and I see the peace offering for what it is.

Now I have a choice.

I can either play the douche and tell Asher to fuck off for the next month.

Or I can take the beer.

I glance at the bottle, the amber brew icy cold in Asher's hand, and let out a self-deprecating snicker. "You're such an asshole."

"I know." He shrugs.

With a grin, I take the bottle.

CHAPTER 3

Asher's relieved. His short bark of laughter hides nothing.

As much as he likes to rile me up, I guess he doesn't want me hating on him.

He takes a seat opposite us and uncaps his own beer. I let him clink it against mine.

He's bound to piss me off again soon, but for now, we'll take things for what they are.

I guess it wasn't him who agreed to the bet. I was the idiot who shook on it, and I was the idiot who then lost at darts.

His only fault was goading me into it.

And maybe that's actually my fault for being stupid enough to fall for his cocky superiority.

"So, how was Offside?" Liam reaches for the chip packet and opens it up, passing it around before munching down on a massive handful.

"Eh." Asher gives a noncommittal shrug. "The usual.

Riley decided it was finally time to try and score the big fish."

"No way," Liam laughs. "He was trying it on with Sonia?"

"You bet."

"How'd he do?"

"No idea. I left while he was still mid-play. We'll no doubt get the update tomorrow. I saw Casey walking out the door with some redhead tucked under his arm."

"He can never resist a redhead."

"I know, right?"

I crack up laughing, the loud sound interrupting their flow of conversation.

"What?" Liam's eyebrows pucker.

"Can't resist a redhead. The guy can't resist *any* kind of pussy. Hair color doesn't make a shit of difference to that guy. He'll walk out of a bar with any girl who catches his eye. The guy's only type is female. That's it."

Asher nods and starts laughing too. "Shit, you're so right, man."

We all sit there grinning, sipping our drinks and shaking our heads over the tattooed playboy, when the door clicks open again, and who should strut in but the one and only.

"That was quick," Asher hassles him.

"Just did it in the back of her car." Casey shrugs. "After that she had to split, so I figured I'd come hang out with you D-bags."

"You mean strut in here and make us all feel like shit

because you were the only one who got some tonight?" Asher arches his brow.

A wide grin stretches across Casey's face as he spins a chair around and straddles it. "You bet your fuckin' asses."

Liam snickers, shoving the chip packet toward him. He takes out a giant handful and scoffs it down before reaching for a beer.

"So, how was it?"

I frown at Asher's question. Why does he ask that shit? I don't want to live vicariously through Casey's sexcapades.

"It was good." His shoulder hitches, but then a smile curls his lips. "Actually, it was fucking epic. She rode me like a cowgirl, and damn if it wasn't hot as shit."

I glance at Liam, who's rolling his eyes.

"She reminded me a lot of my first for some reason. I think it was those cute little sounds she was making."

"Oh yeah?" Asher grins. "And who was your first?"

Casey's eyebrows dip. "I can't even remember her name."

"Dude, you can't remember the name of your first time?" Liam blinks at him in surprise. "You are such a slut."

"I know." He nods, then winks with a smirk.

"How old were you?"

"Eighteen. Summer after graduation."

"You didn't get some in high school?" Now Asher's looking all surprised. "How is that possible? You're like a walking sex machine. I figured you lost it when you were like thirteen."

He lets out a barking laugh, then shrugs again. "It's not like I hadn't tried. I'd done everything but the actual deed. Just needed to find me the right girl."

"Oh yeah, of course. What was her name again?" Asher scoffs, reaching for another beer.

I join him, using the handle of my fork to uncap the bottle.

"I didn't lose it until after high school," I admit.

I have no fucking idea why I just said that, but I did.

And now they're all staring at me, obviously as surprised about me as they were about Casey.

Well, not Liam. He nods like he gets it, and we share a look that only friends with years' worth of history can ever share.

Clearing my throat, I glance at my other roommates. They're staring at me, obviously wanting more deets, and I can't help a small smile.

Shanna Reeves.

That sexy thing gave me the night of my life.

Best damn coach a guy could ask for.

I take a swig from my bottle, my mind wandering back to my freshman year at Nolan U...

CHAPTER 4

Two years earlier...

"Yo! Freshman!"

I spin on the ice and miss the puck that's coming my way like a fucking missile.

It smacks the board behind me and ricochets into my skate before firing toward Henson, who gathers it with a snicker and skates circles around me.

Shit.

Way to make a first impression.

I push off from the wall and head into the middle of the rink where Liam is skating like a pro, playing with the puck like he's been doing it all his life.

Which he has.

We both have, which means I shouldn't be acting like a newbie on the ice.

I grunt, gathering the puck and veering left around Henson, then speeding toward Casey and Asher. Thank God I'm not the only freshman on the team this year. Now I have to make sure I'm not the worst one here.

Focusing on the goal, I follow the drill Coach gave us and manage to hit the net. Thank fuck for that!

"And another! Let's go, let's go, let's go. Pick up the pace, boys!" Coach is yelling from the sidelines, and I do what I'm told, sweat prickling the back of my neck as I try to be the guy he wants on his team.

High school was so much easier than this.

Liam and I shone like stars on our team. I gave hockey everything my senior year. It was a way to cope, to distract myself so I didn't have to face the fact that my mom wasn't around anymore.

She drove me to every hockey practice when I was a kid.

Came to every game.

And now the only thing watching me is her ghost.

I can't decide if that brings me comfort or just makes the grief worse.

Screaming around the back of the goal, I charge at Asher, stealing the puck away from him and making a beeline for the goal. He's on my tail, swearing at me, so I move a little faster, my blades cutting through the ice as I lift my stick and fire away.

The puck rises...and dread floods me like a toxic wave. The angle's wrong. It's gonna—shit!

Hitting the top bar of the goal, the puck pings into the air, becoming a lethal bullet that catches the team captain right on the back of the helmet.

Double shit!

"What the fuck!" He spins around while I wince and try to shrink to half my size.

"Sorry." I raise my glove in apology, but it's too fucking late.

He shakes his head, giving me a pitying frown before skating off the ice to go talk to Coach.

Triple shit, they're gonna cut me.

I fucking deserve it after this wreck of a practice.

Glancing around the rink, I try not to let the stares burn me. Casey is wincing and scratching his shoulder. Liam's wearing this worried face, and some of the guys near the opposite goal have skated into a huddle and are now snickering and no doubt talking about what a shit player I am.

Fuck. What am I doing here?

Mom, I'm sorry. I wanted to make you proud, but—

"Galloway." Coach waves me over, and I share a foreboding look with Liam.

His concerned frown only deepens, and that just makes it worse, so I turn my back on him, trying to lift my chin. Trying to act like I can take this.

I stop by the boards, forcing myself to look Coach in the eye.

He gives me a long hard stare before muttering, "You're better than this, kid." Then he huffs. "Would you stop looking like you just decapitated the guy? He's fine."

I glance at Griffin, whose mouth is now tipped up in a lopsided grin.

Even so, I wince, still feeling like I don't belong here.

"You're done for today." Coach slaps me on the shoulder. "Go shower up and shake it off. Tomorrow, you'll be back, and I want to see the guy I saw lead his high school team like a hockey pro, got it?"

"Yeah," I mumble.

"What?" he barks at me.

"Yes, Coach."

He nods, a silent *That's better.*

Griffin slaps me on the back as I hop over the boards and make my way to the locker room.

I should be relieved I didn't get cut, but that doesn't change the fact that I probably deserve to be.

Shit, I need to up my game.

College is not what I thought it would be.

Liam and I had big dreams of fresh starts, strutting into manhood like we owned the world. We felt like fucking kings as we drove up to Nolan U.

I was finally getting away from the hollow shell that my house had been since Mom died. I was gonna hit college and get me some girls. I was gonna be the new star hockey player. I was gonna play hard, party hard, and live it up.

So far, all I'd managed to do was embarrass myself.

And as for girls...

I shake my head, stripping off my sweaty jersey and honestly wondering if I'm gonna graduate from college with my V-card still intact.

CHAPTER 5

I'm out of the shower by the time Liam trudges into the locker room.

He's giving me his sad smile. The one that tells me he feels my pain and is really sorry that life sucks right now.

I shrug, trying to act like I don't give a shit.

But he sees right through it like he always does.

"I would ask you if you want to go get drunk, but I already know the answer," I mutter, stuffing my clothes into my bag.

He snickers. "I can watch you get drunk if you want."

"Nah." I shake my head.

"Partying it up might be good for you. Blow off some steam. I'll be your DD if you want to hit up a frat house and find some cheap beer."

I give him a halfhearted shrug.

"Maybe we can get one of the seniors to hook us up. Have a quiet beer at the park or something."

Another noncommittal shrug from me makes him sigh. I know he's trying to make me feel better and I'm making it really hard on him, but I don't have the heart to tell him to just shut the fuck up and stop already.

He's my best friend, and he's a good guy.

"Well, I'm not gonna sit around watching you sulk. We need to do *something*." He lightly punches me in the arm. "Maybe I should just get these guys to drag your ass to Offside."

I give in to a snicker as the rest of the team piles into the locker room. I get various looks, most of them accompanied by mocking laughter.

"Nice playing out there, fresh boy."

"There's always one."

"Newbie's got it out for the captain!"

Griffin laughs. "Shut up, you guys. He's gonna buy me a beer to make up for it, right?" Slapping me on the arm, he gives me another one of those grins, and I'm nodding before I can stop myself.

I have no idea why he's being so nice to me when I could have knocked him out cold. Thank fuck he was wearing his helmet.

"Stick around, noob. Let me just shower up."

I sigh and nod, hating the new nickname.

Liam hides a smile behind his hand while Casey doesn't even bother trying to be subtle about it. "Noob. Classic." His laughter is a loud bark, and I could hate him for it if he wasn't such a lovable guy. We only met a few weeks ago, when hockey training kicked in, and I already like him. He's loud and proud and funny. It's a good combo.

Swinging open his locker, he starts arranging his stuff while I keep my eyes on the floor. What the hell else am I gonna do?

Liam showers up quick fast, and he's soon sitting with me while we wait for everyone else.

He's not a drinker. He has his reasons. I think they're dumb, but the one time I tried to tell him that, I thought I'd lost him for life. We figured it out, and I've learned to never bring it up. If he doesn't want to drink, then I have to respect that. Even though I'm convinced he'll never turn into his dad, he doesn't want to hear it.

"So—" Whatever Liam's about to say is cut off by his phone.

He reads the message on the screen, his shoulders slumping.

"What's up?"

"What do you think?" His dark tone and deep scowl tell me right away. "Why can't he just leave them the fuck alone?"

"Do you want me to come?"

"No. Why should your night have to suck too?" He shoots off the bench and snatches his stuff.

I pull the keys for my truck out of my pocket. "My night already sucks. Come on, I'll drive."

"Forget it," he mumbles, holding out his hand. "I can deal with it. I should probably go alone anyway, you know? Mom always hates an audience."

That's true. I wince, thinking about last time and how she shut herself away in her room and wouldn't stop crying or let Liam help her. I'm sure I was part of the reason why.

I give in with a sigh, slapping the keys into his palm and watching him storm out the door.

Shit, I hate his stupid dad. I wish there was more I could do.

I mean, I could just wait in the truck, but I can usually tell when Liam just wants to go on his own, and tonight's definitely one of those times.

Liam's gonna have to drive all the way to Denver just to dish out some hugs and words of assurance to his weepy mother and hysterical sister. Shit, his dad better not have crossed the line again. They've learned to lock the door and let him holler outside the windows, but it all depends how much liquor is flowing through his bloodstream. He better be gone by the time Liam gets there.

Although, if he's not, Liam's a big enough unit to handle it now.

I just don't want him to have to.

But he doesn't want me there. I've tried to fight him on it in the past, but he gets really shitty if I push too hard, and he's already dealing with enough.

Sighing, I dip my head and wonder if this day could get any worse.

"Stop sulking, Galloway." Griffin flicks me with his

towel. "So you screwed up. Everyone does. Get your ass up. Let's go."

"Where are we going?"

The guys behind Griffin laugh, shaking their heads and muttering a few variations of "newbie."

"Do you really need to ask?" Henson winks at me. "It's Offside time, baby!"

The guys cheer, and I trail them out the door.

Griffin turns back to check on me, slowing his pace until we're walking side by side.

"Seriously, dude. Let it go."

"I could have killed you."

He snickers and shakes his head. "It was a freak accident, and I guarantee you're gonna spend the rest of this week focusing overtime on getting that shot right. You'll practice your ass off, and you'll never hit the bar again."

I glance at him, wondering how he knew I had every intention of showing up early tomorrow so I could get some extra hours in.

"I used to be a freshman, too, you know. We all have to deal." He nudges me with his elbow. "And then we have to shake it off."

Following him out of the stadium, I climb into the truck with the rest of the guys.

"Let's get pissed and forget our names!" Leroy hollers.

"Let's get some pussy and forget our names," counters Henson.

I snicker, glad I'm in the back seat. I'm too young to

legally drink, not that it stops me, and never in a million years will I admit to these guys that I'm a virgin.

My mom was too sick for me to think about girls in high school. Like I could go off screwing the cheer squad when my mom was dying in her bed. I spent every spare minute I could with her. Girls were an afterthought... a barely there thought.

But it's been a year now, and the sting of losing her has softened to a dull ache.

College is supposed to be my fresh start, but so far...

I look out the window as we head for Offside, worrying about Liam. Worrying about me and this whole college experience.

It'd be so easy to bail, to head back home to Dad and use the excuse that I need to look after him.

Maybe Liam and I should both be heading home to take care of our families.

Or is that just the world's lamest excuse to avoid the fact that my dreams of kingdom at college have turned to ash?

The reality is I'm a total newbie loser... and everybody knows it.

CHAPTER 6

We get to Offside, and I shove my hands in my pockets, calculating how long it will take me to sprint to my dorm room. I could hide away, distract myself with some *John Wick* or some shit. Heads being blown off sounds like a good way to spend my night. It's gotta be better than standing on the sidelines while these guys get drunk and horny, scoring themselves puck bunnies while I sit here too young to score myself a beer and too inexperienced to score myself one of those hotties by the bar.

Or the pool table.

Or shit, look at the dance floor!

My dick starts twitching, and I clench my jaw, heading for the table that Henson and Griffin are taking over.

My phone dings, and I pull it out of my back pocket.

Liam: Crisis averted. The old man has been picked up by

the cops. I spoke to my mom, and she told me not to come. Sophia's not crying, and they don't want me driving all that way.

Me: You wanna come hang at Offside?

Liam: Nah. I'm gonna go back to the dorm. And don't say you'll join me. Seriously, dude. You need to shake off practice. If I see you back at the dorm before 10, and without a decent story to tell me, I'll be pissed.

I snicker and send him a few emojis to tell him I understand.

Guess I better find myself a decent story.

But what?

Why didn't I shell out for a fake ID? The last one I had was cut in half my first week here. It was some cheap shit that didn't pass muster, and the bouncer at the club gave me a pitiful headshake before destroying it.

Seriously.

I've been through some shit in my time, but I never thought I'd be riding the express train to Loserville.

Standing next to Griffin, I glance around the bar, my eyes catching on a curvy brunette with luscious hair down to her waist and boobs that she's obviously proud of. The tight top she's sporting leaves nothing to the imagination, and her jeans look painted on.

I can't take my eyes off her as she laughs at something her friend said, flicking her hair over her shoulder. Her red, full mouth is stretched into a sexy smile, and my throat's going dry.

"Okay, point at the hottie, big man. Who's got you in a trance?" Henson snaps his fingers in my face.

"Oh. Uh... that one." I raise my chin. There's a bunch of girls over there, so they probably won't know which one I mean. I clarify. "Red shirt."

"Shanna Davies." Griffin smiles. "Damn, she has got to have one of the best racks on campus."

We all stare at her boobs, and she must sense it because her head swivels our way. I'm pretty sure I turn a bright shade of fire engine while she gives us a simpering smirk that makes my dick spring to life under the table.

"Damn. She is one fine honey." Henson's eyeing her up with a look that tells her exactly what he's interested in.

"Leave her be, man." Griffin lightly slaps his arm. "Let noobs have her."

Henson's eyebrow quirks up before he glances over his shoulder at me. "You up for it?"

I swallow, forcing a smile that's probably edgy and pathetic.

Henson grins, swiveling to face me. Resting his elbows on the table, he leans in with a gleam in his eye. "She's a hot ride."

"Really?" I swallow, fisting my hand inside my jacket pocket and feeling so out of my depth that I don't even think a life raft can save me. "You know?"

"Hell yeah, I know. Half the guys in this place do."

My eyes dart to where she's standing. She's talking to her friend again but still obviously aware of our ogling. Her lips are twitching, which tells me she likes it.

"The thing you have to understand about Shanna is that she loves sex." Griffin smiles. "She's a sure thing."

I clear my throat, my shoulder hitching as I figure there's no point going for it now. She's experienced and will see right through me in a heartbeat. After the practice I've endured tonight, I'm not sure I'm up for the humiliation.

"The other thing we all love about that woman"—Henson nudges my elbow—"is that she loves to break in the young colts. That's why we call her Professor Sex. If any chick in his bar can teach you a thing or two, it's her."

I frown at him, but Henson just laughs, slapping my shoulder and heading to the bar.

Shit. Is my virginity that fucking obvious?

Griffin sends me a little wink. "Go for it, man. I dare you."

With a slap to the table, he wanders off, heading for the pool tables. His arm is soon snaking around the waist of some blonde who turns to smile at him. He grins back, all suave and cool. He's like James Bond.

How does he do that?

Shit. The guy's got game.

He makes it look so fucking easy.

Like walking up to a sexy chick and talking to her is no harder than ordering a burger.

Working my jaw to the side, I glance at Shanna again

and am seconds away from bailing when her eyes connect with mine and that sexy little smirk of hers lands right on me.

Yeah, that's right. She's looking my way, and like some siren from the deep, she's calling me toward her.

I'm helpless to stop my body from moving her way.

Looks like I'm not quite done with humiliating myself today. I guess I may as well go down trying to pull off something epic like talking to the hottest woman in this place.

CHAPTER 7

Sweat is beading the back of my neck by the time I reach her.

In a show of mercy, she's moved away from her friends and is standing alone at a high table near the bar.

The tip of her tongue skims the edge of her mouth as I stop beside her and try for a smile.

Shit, what the hell is my mouth doing right now?

She lets out a girlish laugh that tickles my taste buds, and I can't take my eyes off those glossy lips.

I have no idea what I'm supposed to say, but I'm screaming at myself to play it cool.

Cool. Casual. Charming. Sexy.

I want to have the edge of a guy like Maximus from *Gladiator* with the charm of Mr. Bond.

But of course, when I rest my elbow on the table and clear my throat, my brain turns to oatmeal and all I can come up with is... "So, did it hurt?"

Holy fuck, I did not just say that!

You're going for cool, not moronic, you big douche!

She snickers and turns to face me, her boobs squishing together and practically spilling out of her top. "Really?"

I have no way of recovering from this, so just end up sputtering, "Well, I mean... I... you definitely fell from heaven, right?"

She shakes her head, her look almost pitiful. "Try again."

"Again? Okay... uh..." I scratch the back of my head. "Are you tired?"

Biting her lips together, she fails to hold back her laughter. "Nope."

"Come on, really? Because you've been running through my mind all day."

"That is so bad." She laughs, shaking her head.

Well, her upper lip's not curling and she's still standing here, so I figure I may as well ride the Loserville train right into the station.

"Do you want me to try again?" I wince.

"Okay, one more." She holds up her finger, her glossy red nail shining at me when she points it in my face. "And this one better be good."

I nod, finding this embarrassing game kind of entertaining. I don't know why, but I made her laugh, so that's gotta be good, right?

Searching my brain, I try to think of the cheesiest,

worst pickup line and quickly settle for... "Did you just come out of the oven?"

She throws her head back, her musical laughter making me feel like I just won a prize. "You really think I'm that hot?"

"Baby, you're scorching."

Oh, she liked that. Her face is telling me so.

My body suddenly feels like an inferno.

"Okay, my little snack." Her hand lands on my shoulder, her sparkling eyes luring me in. "Let me teach you a thing about sexy girls like me."

Dry throat is kicking in big-time, but I manage to rasp, "Oh yeah? What's that?"

Her red lips twitch, rising into a slow smile as she leans toward me, her breath tickling my ear when she whispers, "You can just start with hi and tell me your name."

Leaning back, I drink her in, hoping she can see how freaking hot I think she is before smiling and managing to throw a little husk into my voice. "Hi."

She grins. "Hey there."

"I'm Ethan."

Her look of appreciation makes my insides sizzle as she extends her hand. I take it, giving it a light squeeze as we shake. "I'm Shanna."

My brain kind of shuts down as her gaze heats with a bone-melting look and that tongue of hers glides across her lips. "Wanna get out of here?"

"Really?" My voice breaks. I can't help it.

She laughs like I'm adorable. "Oh, we're gonna have so much fun tonight."

Biting her bottom lip, she turns away from me, shouting out a goodbye to her friends before taking my hand and leading me out of Offside.

I'm reeling.

Like seriously.

What the hell just happened?

I'm walking out of the bar with my personal wet dream, and she's acting like I'm not a total douche nugget with the cheesiest lines in history.

It felt way too easy.

She must be into my boyish charm or something.

Damn. I hope it's enough, because if I'm going to lose my V-card to anyone... I want it to be her.

I better be man enough to do it, because this is gonna be one hell of a story to tell Liam.

CHAPTER 8

She drives her Prius like a Formula One racer, and we screech to a stop outside a big house on the edge of campus.

"Nice place," I murmur.

She shrugs. "I'm a sorority girl."

"Are we on Greek Row or something?" My eyebrows rise.

Her giggle is soft and playful. "Something like that." Those glossy lips curve into a sexy grin, and I act before I can stop myself.

Cupping her cheek, I lean across the car and plant my lips on hers.

She meets my pressure, her supple lips molding against mine as she threads her fingers into my hair, then licks my bottom lip.

I groan and open my mouth, her sexy tongue greeting mine with an eagerness that's pretty damn encouraging.

She wants me.

This hot-cake, Professor Sex, wants me bad.

It's a major confidence booster. Her sweet moan sends a spark firing down to my groin, and I'm seconds away from flipping her seat back and doing it in the car.

As if she can read my mind, she pulls away with a laugh. "Come on, hotshot. Let's go inside."

I adjust my jeans, which only makes her laugh again, before following her out of the car. The door's already unlocked, and she waltzes through the main entrance, waving at a few girls lounging on a sofa before grabbing my hand and pulling me upstairs.

A wolf whistle floats up behind us, and I grin over my shoulder, catching the eye of a cute blonde who grins at me like I'm eye candy.

Shit, this is a whole new ball game.

Maybe college is my fresh start.

"This way." Shanna drags me down the hallway and into a room near the end. It's big with an ensuite and a king-sized bed.

"Whoa," I murmur.

"I know." She dumps her bag on the bed and spins to face me. "It's the privilege of being a senior... and sorority president."

"Sorority... president."

"Yes." She dips her hip. "I love my Gamma Phi sisters. This place has been a lifesaver during my college years, and the least I could do was lead the charge my final year."

"Impressive." I nod. "Must keep you busy."

"It does." She flicks off her heels, dropping down to her bare feet and losing a couple inches. "And entertained."

Her body is lithe and catlike as she walks toward me. I'm mesmerized by the sway of her hips. My hands land on them as soon as she's close enough.

"You know what else is entertaining?" She rises on her toes, her tits brushing my chest as her luscious lips skim over mine. "You."

Fisting my shirt, she pulls me to the bed, spinning me around so my knees hit the edge and I flop back on the mattress.

I land with an "Oomph" before rising on my elbows so I can watch her straddle me.

"So..." She starts tying her hair up in a ponytail like she's preparing for a workout. "What do you know?"

"What do I... know?" I frown up at her.

"Come on, Mr. Cheesy Pickup Lines, it's obvious you're kind of new at this whole seduction thing. So, tell me... what have you done before? You can obviously kiss." Her eyebrows wiggle as she licks her lips. "What else are you good at it?"

I can't stop my wince fast enough, but that seems to please her somehow.

Biting her bottom lip, she tips her head and lets out this sound that's half moan, half cry of triumph before whipping off her shirt and unclasping her bra so fast I've barely had time to blink.

Two large, luscious boobs are the only thing in my vision.

I reach for them, drawn by a power I can't counter. They barely fit inside my hands. Giving them a light squeeze, I enjoy her soft murmur of approval, then brush my thumbs over her nipples.

"Yes," she whispers. "Now kiss them. Suck them. Lick them like a lollipop."

She doesn't have to tell me twice. I lurch upright, running my hand up her back while I suck her left nipple into my mouth.

Holy shit, she tastes delicious.

Her whimpers of approval spur me on as my lips and tongue do their best to make her feel good. It must be working, because she's panting, gripping the back of my hair, and whispering words of encouragement.

"Yes, suck me again, baby. That's good."

I squeeze and suck and lick until she's pushing me away from her. I've left a glossy sheen on her skin, and I watch her boobs jiggle as she starts yanking at my clothing. I'm soon shirtless and lying back while she returns the favor, her tongue painting circles over my chest as she inches down my body.

The clink of my belt buckle and zip of my fly nearly make me pop on the spot.

Holy shit, this is actually happening.

Her long nails dip beneath the band of my boxers, and she lets out a satisfied laugh. "Oh, hello."

She must like what she sees. I want to give her a cocky

smile or say something smart, but I'm concentrating too hard on making this last.

I've spanked the monkey plenty of times, but this is different.

I've never had someone else do it for me. I've never been inside a chick before. I've never had glossy lips and a hot tongue turning my dick into a popsicle.

Holding my breath, I wonder if she's going to do just that as she orders me to lift my hips so she can pull off my clothes.

Tugging the jeans off my ankles, she stands back and stares down at me, crossing her arms beneath her boobs and eyeing me up like I'm sexy.

"Nice," she murmurs. "Very nice."

Unbuttoning her jeans, she shimmies them off her hips, and I sit up, wondering how we're gonna do this. Will she sit on me? Or does she want to go on her back? Or—

"Now..." She pulls open her nightstand drawer and grabs a bottle of hand lotion. "I don't do BJs. Some guys get a little pissy about that, but I don't like doing them, and I have other ways to make you feel just as good." She grins at me as she squeezes a mound of cream into her hands. Rubbing them together, she kneels in front of me, her eyes sparkling as she grips my steel rod.

I suck in a breath. "Cold."

"It'll warm up soon enough, baby." She starts pumping my dick like a piston, the soft suction sounds creating a weird rhythm as she sends my senses into orbit.

Holy fuck, this feels so good.

How the hell am I going to last until sex?

Unless this is sex and I'm not actually going to be doing it with her tonight.

I should still be grateful for this, though, right?

Fuck. I can't think straight.

My dick is having a party. The slick cream and her deft fingers and—shit, she's cupping my balls and sucking my pecs. I'm gonna blow.

I'm gonna fucking blow.

I let out a strangled cry as my body convulses, and I don't even have time to warn her before I spurt into her hands. My dick keeps twitching, firing cum like a fountain. She sits back, pumping me some more and watching the white goop land on my straining abs. I let out another garbled sound that might be words, I really don't know. My brain is incoherent mush as my body does a final shudder.

She grins like this is a win while my expression crumples.

"S-Sorry," I mutter.

"What are you apologizing for?"

I shrug, unable to look at her. "I didn't mean to... I was hoping to..."

She giggles, standing up and reaching out to me. "It's not over yet, McDreamy. I've still got some plans for you." Snatching my hand, she pulls me off the bed. "It's my turn now, so let's take a shower and I'll show you what I want."

Her eyebrows wiggle, and I follow her to the en suite, my heart still racing after my orgasm.

There's more?

My stomach clenches with a giddy hiccup.

Fuck yeah!

There's more!

CHAPTER 9

The glass starts to steam as the hot water hits the tiles beneath us. Pulling out her hair tie, Shanna dips her head beneath the spray, and I have to kiss that long neck of hers.

Skimming my lips across her skin, I close my eyes against the spray and enjoy her moans as I suck and nibble my way down to her breasts again.

She cups the back of my head. "Yeah, baby. That feels good."

"What do you want?" I manage. "How do I make you feel even better."

She spreads her legs, and I watch the water cascade down her silky skin. "Touch me." Her finger trails over her stomach and down to her pussy. She circles the top, letting out a moan as she shows me what she wants.

Running my hand down her curves, I brush my

knuckles over her fingers, and she moves aside, letting me take over.

Guiding my fingers to the exact place she wants, I start spinning circles, and it really gets her going. Her pants become sharp and fast, these moans building in her throat and coming out as little puffs.

"That good?" I whisper in her ear before sucking her lobe into my mouth.

"Yeah," she whimpers.

"How do I give you more?" I run my finger down her slit, dipping it between her folds. "Is that good?"

"Yes." Her breath catches. "I like that."

I push my finger farther inside her, and she groans again. Scraping my teeth lightly down her jaw, I keep going, circling that sweet spot with my thumb while dipping my finger into her soft, warm center.

Drawing her nipple into my mouth again, I enjoy the way her moans get louder and faster, her fingers fisting my hair as I obviously send her to the edge.

This is fucking fantastic.

I love what I'm doing to her right now.

Making her feel good is like winning the Stanley Cup. Maybe even better.

Dropping farther, I start kissing her stomach and finally land on my knees. Her pussy is right there, calling to me, and I go to brush my tongue between the folds.

"You don't have to if you don't want to." Her voice is soft and breathy.

I glance up, the water pelting my face until she shifts the showerhead. "Is it okay if I want to?"

"Yeah, I just don't expect it when I'm not willing to return the favor."

"You don't have to return anything to me." I grin. "I want to taste every inch of you."

Her jaw quivers as her lips part, and then she's brushing her teeth over her bottom lip and I'm feeling like a fucking king.

Gently parting her folds, I lick a line up her pussy, and her groan of ecstasy makes my dick so hard it hurts.

Lifting her leg over my shoulder, she opens herself even more to me, and I enjoy my taste of heaven. My tongue takes the place of my fingers while I grip her thighs, and then she's moaning again, crying out like this is too fucking good as her body starts to strain and shudder.

"Touch my clit. Touch my clit." The words come out in an urgent rush, and I instinctively move, knowing what she means without having to ask.

Sucking her clit between my lips, I feel her walls start to break, and then I glide my finger inside her once more, going deep until I hit a spot that makes her spasm.

She lets out a guttural moan as her muscles clench my finger and the orgasm rips right through her. She grips my shoulders, her body going taut as her cries of ecstasy fill the shower, bouncing off the glass and filling the space. It's surround sound pleasure, and it's sexy as hell.

"Holy shit," she whispers, pushing me away from her and snapping off the water.

I stand, checking her expression to make sure we're still good.

She leans against the wall, panting and gaping at me. The water drips slowly from the showerhead, but all I can see are the droplets on her naked body, gliding a path over her curves. I'm struggling to breathe, trying to figure out what's going to happen next.

But then she lets out this deep laugh that reverberates off the tiles.

Her tongue skims her bottom lip as she eyes me up, and before I know what's happening, her mouth hits mine with a hunger that's intense.

I match her fervor, gripping her body to mine and squeezing her firm ass. Those sweet cheeks fit perfectly into my palms, and I pull her flush against me, loving the way her boobs squish into my chest. My steel rod pokes her stomach, begging to be played with again.

"I need you in me now," she whispers. Again with the breathy urgency. It's so fucking hot.

Shoving open the shower door, she pulls me out onto the tiles and wrenches open the bathroom drawer. She tears the condom packet with her teeth, and I stand there panting as she rolls it onto me.

This is happening.

It's fucking happening.

Dropping to the floor, she spreads her legs and

beckons me to join her. My muscles are twitching, aching with anticipation as I lower myself over her.

The tiles are cool against my knees, and I worry about her lying on this cold floor, but she doesn't seem to notice.

"I need you," she whimpers, guiding me over her.

I line myself up, grateful when she grabs my dick and helps me aim. My tip lands between her folds and the hot oasis that awaits me.

"Now," she begs.

And I thrust.

It's fucking mind-blowing, the best sensation I have ever experienced in my life.

Her hot core wraps around me, drawing me in, and I instinctively thrust again, going even deeper.

"Yes. Shit, yes!" She's panting and spurring me on, her leg rising over my hip, her heel digging into my ass.

I go for it, setting a fast pace that she seems to enjoy.

My body and brain have disconnected as I become aware of only one thing. The way this feels. Her heat. Her lusty energy wrapping around me.

There's this power building inside me. It's an orgasm, I know it is, but it's next level. Rising on my arms, I plant my palms on the floor and bury myself inside her, thrusting hard and fast until this energy is an all-consuming fire.

She lets out a cry, her head tipping back as her pussy milks me in these heady spasms that set off a rocket inside me.

Another hard thrust and an explosion of pleasure courses through me.

I jerk and keep thrusting, emptying myself into her as the burning energy starts to drain. After a final push to the hilt, I go still, straining inside her until my limbs turn to limp noodles.

Flopping over her, I try to hold my weight on my arms so I don't squash her. Our hearts are racing, our breaths bursting in each other's ears.

"Well, that was..." She shakes her head, panting against my cheek. "You are... you are no noob."

"Huh?" I lean back so I can look down at her.

"When I first saw you tonight, I thought I'd be breaking in a total newbie. I like to do that, you know? Kind of like a service to all those poor guys out there who don't think they have what it takes."

"That's, um... really nice of you."

Her lips quirk into a proud smirk before she gazes up at me, her finger trailing down my cheek. "You, though. You are no noob."

"Actually—" I wince. "—I am. I mean, you're my... first."

Her eyebrows rise with surprise, and then she tips her head back, laughter making her body shake beneath me. "Holy shit. I can't wait to see what you'll be like with a little practice. You..." She tips her head to look me in the eye. "You are gonna be Nolan U's sex god. Shit, you already are."

"Sex god?" I can't help a smug smile.

She giggles, pulling me down for a deep kiss. "My personal Eros. Not sure I'm ready to share you with the world yet."

"I don't have a problem with that." I wink at her, and she kisses me again.

CHAPTER 10

Present day...

"Eros? Are you fucking kidding me?" Casey barks out a laugh.

Meanwhile, Asher's looking skeptical. "No way." He shakes his head. "She actually called you a sex god?"

"That is what Eros means." And here comes my smug smile again. But come on, how can I not be smug? I lost my V-card to the hottest girl on campus, and she didn't realize I was a virgin. It was a fucking epic first time... and second time, and third, fourth, and fifth.

Liam raises his chin at me. "I remember Shanna. You guys dated for a while, right?"

"Not really. We just hooked up for a couple months...

until she fell in love with that football player." I make a face. I can't help it.

I was on the verge of falling in love with the sex queen, and she went and ditched me for a wide receiver. Apparently, they're married with baby number two already on the way. Talk about a life changer.

"I think I remember that," Casey mumbles. "It was her high school sweetheart or something. He showed up on campus with those roses, and all the girls went gaga."

"Yup." I pop the *P*. "He just waltzed back in and stole her heart all over again. I had no shot."

"Did you really want one?" Liam gives me a quizzical frown.

I shrug. It's not like I have a rep for serious relationships. In fact, since then, I've had none. I did date another sorority girl for a short while, but it quickly became clear to me that casual was the way to go, and I'm very open about that with all the girls I hook up with.

"Well, sex god, that's a pretty epic first time." Casey raises his beer bottle, and I tap mine against it.

"Thanks, man. She taught me everything I know." I grin, taking a swig of beer and wondering if she calls her hubby "my personal Eros" too.

Probably.

But that's okay.

For a little while, I was hers. And I don't mind the name.

It's better than noob and douche nugget... but maybe not as cool as Captain Hero.

I hide my smile behind my beer bottle as my mind flashes back to the sassy-mouthed shorty I met last night.

"So, what's your story, then? Do you just prowl the campus at night, looking for lonely girls to rescue? Let me guess, you're a vigilante, right? What's your code name? The Jock? Tall Man? Captain Hero?"

I snorted. "Those are the worst hero names ever. Have you even read a comic book before?"

"Hey, I happen to love Marvel and DC movies, okay?"

"And Captain Hero was the best you could come up with?"

"Gimme a break. I'm working on the fly here." Her lips stretched into a grin, and something inside me hitched.

Damn, I want to see her again.

And shitballs, I can't.

Not with this stupid bet hanging over me.

I've got to avoid that sexy shorty like she's forbidden fruit.

Which she is. Oh man, I bet she tastes sweet too.

Stop it. You can't have her. End of story.

The black-and-white directive should bring me some relief. It's an easy rule to follow, right? Just stay away from her. But... fuck, that's disappointing.

Taking another swig of beer, I try not to think about my mystery girl, but it's a losing game.

Click this link to start reading Ethan & Mikayla's romance:

www.katyarcher.com/the-forbidden-freshman

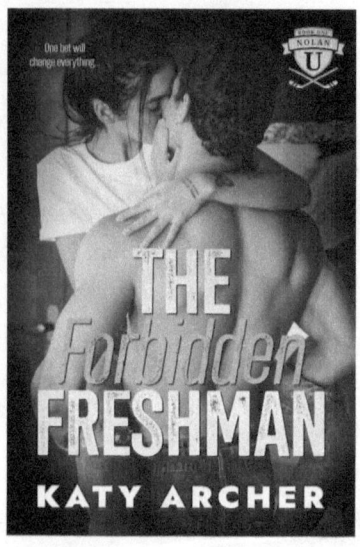

Once you've done that, you can keep reading to find out how Liam lost his V-card to one of his best friends in high school...

LIAM

THE BEST FRIEND

CHAPTER 11

Eros.

Sex god.

Of course Ethan scored a name like that.

Of course his first time was epic.

I'm not saying things always fall in his favor, but he's got a way of turning coal into diamonds. Girls love him.

And I'm damn sure it's because Shanna put in a good word for the guy.

Sex god.

I shake my head, my smile fading as I think about my first time. Shit, there was nothing godly about that ordeal. My wince is impossible to hide, and of course Ethan notices.

"What are you cringing about?" He swivels to face me, leaning his forearms on the table.

His adamant look tells me I'm gonna have to spill the tea or he'll dog me all night.

What is this? A fucking sorority?

"You better not be thinking about your first time," Asher mutters. "With a look like that, it can't be good."

"It wasn't." I swallow, then snap my eyes shut, wishing I hadn't said anything.

"Seriously?" Casey sits forward, too, so now I'm facing the V-card inquisition.

Well, shit. There's no getting out of this now.

I let out a self-deprecating chuckle. "Seriously."

"What was wrong with it?" Casey asks. "You fire off too early or something?"

"No." My cheeks are starting to burn. "But I sure as shit didn't know what I was doing. Neither of us did."

"Aw. Two little virgins losing it together." Asher puts on a sticky-sweet smile, then pouts. "How cute."

Ethan snickers, sharing a quick look with the other two before asking, "How old were you?"

"Fifteen."

"No way." His eyebrows pop high.

"Nearly sixteen. It was the end of sophomore year."

Ethan swallows, and I know he's thinking about his mom. His voice is soft and husky as he mumbles, "You never told me."

I shrug, avoiding the real reason I didn't want to burden him. "It's not the kind of story you want to brag about."

"Okay, now you have to tell us." Casey wriggles in his seat like he's getting comfortable, leaning his broad chest against the back of the chair.

And now I'm having major insta-regret over saying anything. Fuck, I'm regretting my wince. I'm usually pretty good and keeping things on the down-low. I'm the King of Calm. Mr. Unflappable. The guy who knows how to smile when his insides are raging.

But I just had to go fucking wince, didn't I?

"Who was it with?" Ethan picks at the label on his beer bottle. "Did I know her?"

My face bunches as I wince yet again.

His expectant gaze is a silent demand I can't deny, so I huff, "Emily Myers."

"Emily My—Emily?" His voice pitches in surprise. "We treated her like a sister, man. You seriously bumped uglies with her? When? How did that happen?"

Crap on a stick.

I run a hand down my face.

How did I get myself into this situation?

I'm sharing my V-card story with a bunch of dudes and shocking the hell out my best friend at the same time.

I swore I'd never tell anyone about my first time, but I know damn well they won't let this slide. I'll either get pranked until I capitulate or they'll pin me to the floor and dead-arm me until I give in.

Looks like this is actually happening.

Liam Carlisle is finally telling the truth about his first time...

CHAPTER 12

Five years earlier...

I shove my bike into the stand and throw the chain around the wheel. When the padlock sticks, I growl and finally snap it shut with a grunt.

The sky is crystal clear today, and all I can do is glare up at it, frustrated that everything around me seems so normal, like the world doesn't know a storm is brewing. It's dark and black and it'll leave carnage in its wake, and there's not a fucking thing I can do to stop it.

The storm is called Bobby Carlisle.

Hurricane Bobby is a dangerous beast. When he's drunk, he's feral. When he's had a shitty day at work, it shakes the house.

And I can always feel it coming.

Like last night, when he slammed the door shut and stormed into the kitchen, not even acknowledging anyone as he wrenched open the refrigerator and snatched out a can.

"Mi amor?" Mama's words came out short and shaky as she wiped her hands on her apron and kept her back against the counter. "Are you okay?"

He grunted and spun to face us, eyeing us all with a curled upper lip before muttering something about taking a shower.

Mama looked down at the floor, sucking in a tired breath before glancing at me. She didn't have to say anything. I knew what she was thinking. And so I did what she told me to. I slapped my textbook shut and smiled at my baby sister.

"You up for ice cream?"

"Really?" She bobbed in her seat, her dimples showing.

I forced out a laugh because that's what Mama needed me to do. "Sure. Then maybe we can go to Abuela's house for dinner."

"I'll call and let her know." Mama spun back around and continued with the dishes. "Can you, uh... can you text Maria and tell her to stay at her friend's house for the night?"

I winced but nodded. "Go put your shoes on." I pointed at Sophia, and she jumped down from the stool and disappeared. I walked into the kitchen, resting my hand on Mama's back. "I don't want to leave you."

"I'll be fine," she whispered. "It's better this way. Safer. I'll watch my step."

"Don't let him touch you."

She turned to me with glassy eyes, a look of hopelessness crossing her face before she cupped my cheek and gave me a watery smile. "The main thing is that he doesn't touch my babies."

"Come with us."

"That'll only make him worse. He needs me here."

I grunted, not even bothering to hide my contempt for the man I'm supposed to call Dad. He's an asshole. I wish I didn't have his blood running through my veins. I wish I could dig his DNA out of my system and be free of him.

"Liam." Mama smoothed her hand down my face. "It'll be okay. Bring Sophia back before her bedtime and sneak upstairs. Just avoid him as best you can, and I'll keep him distracted."

"Mama—"

"Go." She pointed toward the front door.

"I—"

"Go."

With a huff, I turned and did as she told me.

When I brought Sophia back at eight, Bobby was asleep in front of the TV. Mama's face wasn't black and blue, so it felt like a win.

But the storm is brewing.

Hurricane Bobby is going to sweep through our house any day now, and my petite Mama is going to stand like a fierce lioness, taking the brunt of the storm while I pull my sisters into hiding.

I hate it so fucking much.

I'm bigger now. Maybe not as tall or as strong, but I could fight him. I'm getting tougher every damn day. It wouldn't be like last time. I could hold my ground. Maybe I could turn the tables and crack a few of *his* ribs.

Clenching my jaw, I stalk into school, forcing a smile when I'm greeted by some cheerleaders at the front door, then raising my hand to give Donna and her brother, Josh, a wave.

"Hey guys."

"'Sup, Liam."

I slap Josh's hand as I walk past.

Nobody knows about the storms in my house.

My neighbors might, but they've never done anything to stop them.

When it comes to school, I like to keep things quiet. I have to. Can't have the gossip mill turning with shit about my family. Maria's a senior this year. She doesn't want our private nightmare circulating. We made a pact to keep our mouths shut, and even Sophia has done her part, as far as I'm aware.

In truth, five years ago, we made a pact to leave his ass.

But Mama won't go.

She loves him.

I don't understand why, but... she does. Even after all the bullshit, she stays with him. Sometimes it makes me want to judge her. How can six red roses make up for a bloody lip?

But somehow they do.

Somehow they're laughing together three days later, acting like two teens in love.

Love.

It's so fucking complicated.

I don't know if I ever want it in my life.

Shit, I don't know what I want.

Maybe I can figure it out in college.

If I can just get there, maybe I'll have a chance of getting on with my life and freeing myself of this bullshit.

"Hey, man."

I glance up and spot Ethan leaning against my locker.

His eyes are dark, the gray smudges underneath reminding me that my life is not as shitty as his right now.

I hold in my sigh and force a smile. "Hey, bro." Taking his hand, I give him a hug, patting his shoulder twice before stepping back. "How's your mom?"

He swallows, his forehead crinkling as he looks to the ground. "Her hair started falling out last night. She was just... running her fingers through it, you know? And these... these big clumps just fell away." He clenches his jaw, his nostrils flaring.

I don't know what to say when he tells me this stuff.

How do you make someone feel better when the reality is so incredibly shit?

"Fuck cancer," I mumble.

Ethan nods, sniffing and obviously trying not to lose it.

His mom started chemo two weeks ago. She's been sick for a while but did her best to hide it. She didn't want to make a fuss, but by the time Ethan's father forced her to the doctor, the cancer had already started spreading. They're hitting it hard in the hopes of killing those lecherous cells, but no one's sure how it'll go down.

I pat his shoulder, trying to make him feel better. I'm about to conjure up some lame-ass line like "She'll be okay."

But what the hell do I know?

I want her to be okay.

Shit, she has to be.

Ethan's mom is the best. I adore her. Everybody does. She can't die.

Oh fuck. What if she does?

I can't breathe for a second as I let that thought ride through me.

"Hey, guys." Emily bops up to us.

Yes, bops. The girl doesn't know how to walk. She's a dancer, and ever since I've known her, she's always pranced, bopped, or skipped her way through life.

Her cheerful grin is impossible to resist, and I smile back, grateful for the distraction.

"'Sup, Em." I lightly nudge her shoulder.

Ethan and I don't want to drag our little buddy down, so we've stayed kind of tight-lipped over the whole cancer thing. She knows Ethan's mom is sick but doesn't know the extent of it, and hell will freeze over before I ever let her in on my home life.

Emily's too sweet and happy to bring down that way.

She's like our little mascot. Always coming to our hockey games. Always sitting with us at lunch, helping us with our homework, and beating our asses at *Madden*. I don't know how the fuck she does that, but the girl can game.

She's been our friend since sixth grade, and although our group has grown and expanded since then, she's always been a part of it.

And I'm pretty sure she always will be.

CHAPTER 13

The library is humming with that usual quiet buzz—the tick of the ancient clock on the wall, the shuffle of papers, the tapping of laptop keys, and the odd cough or sniff from a student.

I settle into my seat and spot Kaylee and Michael on the other side of the table. They're whispering to each other, her giggling while he leans in close and says something right into her ear.

Her cheeks turn pink, her teeth scraping her bottom lip before she leans back and gives him a look that could set fire to an igloo.

Oh yeah, that guy is getting some after school today.

I shake my head with a little snicker, wondering what that will feel like. It hasn't happened for me yet, but I'm only fifteen, and it's not like I have a girlfriend. I've had the note-passing relationship in seventh grade and a few slobbery make-out sessions at the freshman winter dance and Shona McNally's movie night, but no girl has called me hers or walked the hallways holding my hand.

One day I think I want that.

As long as it doesn't turn into the toxic bullshit my parents having going on. But that's on me, right? I just won't turn into my old man. Even if it means never touching a drop of alcohol. I'll do whatever it takes not be him.

I spot couples in the street sometimes, and they look so happy, so into each other. I even saw this old couple last week who were holding hands like two teenagers, sitting at the bus stop and laughing together like the rest of the world didn't exist.

Am I being a romantic sap thinking that kind of stuff is cool?

Will it ever happen for me?

I don't know. But having a girl who looks at me like I'm the only guy in the world... that'd be kinda nice.

Kinda nice?

Shit. I need to stop watching girly movies with Maria.

"Hey," Emily whispers in my ear.

I jerk and turn to look at her. Her pixie face smiles down at me as she tucks a lock of mouse-brown hair behind her ear. She's been growing it out since her disastrous decision to cut it super short two years ago. I think she'd just watched "You've Got Mail"—that old movie with Meg Ryan and Tom Hanks. Anyway, she thought Meg's hair was adorable and wanted the same.

She hated it the second she walked out of the salon

and ran to Ethan's place, where we and his mom spent the next two hours convincing her she looked awesome.

Just quietly, I like her hair longer way better. It's down past her shoulders now, and today she has it braided. Her fine hair is falling out of the braid, but it's kinda cute.

She's cute, so it's a perfect match.

"Hey. What's up?" I whisper.

She slips into a chair beside me, flashing me her bright smile before checking where the librarian is.

"I'm just here to study." She pulls out her books, and I try to focus back on the novel I'm meant to be dissecting. I need to find a quote that will prove my point about sexism in the twentieth century. It should be easy enough to find a good one.

Scanning the page, I spot something usable and am about to scribble it down when a note lands on my binder.

I glance at Emily, who winks at me, then turns back to her work with this blushing smile that's just plain weird.

I narrow my eyes at her before grabbing the note and unfolding it.

Will you be my first?

I frown, tipping my head and trying to figure out what she means.

I mean, it sounds like she wants me to be her first, but that can't be right because we're just friends. And not the flirty kind who say to everyone they're friends but act like they're more. We're seriously... just friends. She's like a sister to Ethan and me.

Nudging her elbow with mine, I hold up the note and mouth, "What?"

Her eyes bulge, and she taps on the scrap of paper in my hand.

My head jolts back, my eyes darting around the library to make sure no one's watching before I lean in and softly whisper, "Are you serious?"

She nods once, like this is enough of an explanation.

"What?" I say again, because what the hell else am I supposed to say?

Letting out a soft sigh, she turns to face me, our noses practically touching before she leans back to eyeball me. "Why not?"

My mouth pops open as I struggle to find the words. All I manage is a croaky "Why?"

"Because," she whispers, "you're one of my best friends. And it's not like I can ask Ethan right now. His mom's super sick, and I don't want to bother him with it."

"But... Em, we're..." I frown and shake my head. "We're just friends."

"I know. Exactly." Her head bobs. "We're friends. You're safe. I can trust you."

That's nice and all, but... "We're not in love with each other. We're not dating. We're not a couple."

"What has love got to do with it? And besides, I do love you."

My head jolt backs so fast, she ends up giggling.

We get a sharp "Shh!" from the table next to us, and I hunch over while Emily leans in to whisper, "I mean, I love you like a friend, and that's enough for me. I don't want my first time to be with some guy I'm trying to impress. I want to get it out of the way with someone I know really well so I don't embarrass myself later."

I shake my head, my mind reeling as I try to make sense of this proposal.

This is fucking insane.

Leaning away from her, I do a slow blink, then look down at my textbook before rising from my chair and walking for the stacks.

I don't know why, but I just have to move away from this bizarre conversation.

But of course, the chair behind me scraps against the floor, and I hear Em's boppy little footsteps right behind me.

CHAPTER 14

I keep walking until I reach the back corner of the library where we can talk without glares and curious glances being fired at us.

Turning to face her, I raise my hand before she can take another step closer.

"Em, this is crazy."

"I know, right?" She grins, her eyes sparkling with excitement. She stops, looks around, and I see the first flash of uncertainty skitter across her face. "So... do you want to do it, like, here, because—"

"No. I don't want to do it here," I softly growl. "I don't think we should do it *at all*."

Her expression drops like I've just offended her. "Why not?"

"Because... like I just said before, we're not together that way."

"But we're friends."

"Yeah, *just* friends. I don't understand why you'd choose me for this. Unless, I mean... do you like me? Is this some kind of roundabout way of saying you... I mean, do you love me as more than just a friend or something?"

She shrugs while my heart does this weird twist in my chest. "I don't *not* like you."

Okay, so that's a no. She's not into me like I'm her guy. She just wants to use me for—

"Look, I figure it like this. Losing my V-card is a big deal, and I want it to be with someone I trust."

"Shouldn't it be with someone you love?"

She frowns at me like I'm weird. "You watch way too many romance movies, dude."

My face puckers as I cross my arms with a sigh. "I know. It's Maria's fault."

Crossing her arms to mirror mine, she gives me a droll look. "You don't *have* to watch them with her."

I have no response to that, so I clamp my lips shut and stare at the rows of books instead.

"Come on, Liam. Just think about it. Trust is more valuable to me than love. I want to do it with someone who makes me feel safe, and you always do. When I do get a boyfriend, I want to look like I know what I'm doing." Her expression buckles with desperation. "With you, I can just be myself, and we can figure it out together. It's gonna be awkward and embarrassing, and I want to pick someone who I can handle that with." She points at my chest. "You've seen me with gum in my hair, plus you were the one who told me that day when I'd tucked my skirt into my underwear. I've seen you with your fly down, I was right next to you that time you farted during our algebra test, *and* I always tell you when you have food stuck in your teeth. We can trust each other." She lightly slaps my arm with the back of her hand. "Come on. It's a good idea. Don't you want to get over this big V-card hurdle and at least know how it all works before you get yourself a serious girlfriend?"

"I—" Flicking my hands up, I let them flop back against my thighs. "I don't know."

She sighs, her shoulders slumping as this vulnerable look pulls her lips south. "You don't want me? Am I not attractive or—"

"It's not that," I rush out. "You're beautiful, okay? It's just... it'll change everything between us. What if it's awkward and—"

"I've already said I'm expecting it to be awkward." Her voice pitches. "That's why I want you. If it's with a boyfriend or something, it'll be so much worse. But with us... afterward, we'll still be friends and—"

The bell rings, cutting her off, and I can't deny the relief that pulses through me.

Shoving her hands in her hoodie pockets, she looks up at me with those big eyes of hers and smiles. "Just think about it, okay?"

I nod, because I'm not sure what else I'm supposed to do, then watch her walk away.

For the first time ever, I check out her ass, tucked

away in a tight pair of jeans, and my stupid brain actually wonders what it would feel like in my hands.

Snapping my eyes shut, I shake my head, clearing my throat and trying to get the image of me doing Emily out of my brain.

CHAPTER 15

Emily's request haunts me for the rest of the day.

Am I just being a douche about this?

A girl has asked me to have sex with her. I should be all over that shit.

Shouldn't I?

I don't fucking know.

It just feels wrong somehow. Like we're crossing into uncharted territory that's dangerous. Life altering. And not necessarily in a good way.

Wrenching my locker open, I shove the books inside and figure out what I need for tonight. Homework is piling up as the end of year draws near. Shit, I wish hockey season was still in full swing. I could use the distraction. The excuse.

But the season ended a month or so ago. We played pretty well. Missed out on the finals by one freaking goal. Coach said we still have plenty to be proud of though.

Next year will be our year.

Bring it on.

I'm gonna skate with everything I've got.

Slapping my locker closed, I turn in time to see Ethan approaching.

Should I tell him what Em said to me?

Will it freak him out?

Will he agree with me?

I open my mouth to try and put some words together, but then he pulls out his phone and the expression on his face changes.

He goes from sad to frowning, and not a confused frown but an "oh shit" one. I'm still not used to seeing any kind of frown on him at all. Ever since I've known him, he's been the happy, confident, "the world's my oyster" kind of guy. But then his mom got sick, and everything changed. It's like the Earth snapped its fingers and Ethan became someone else.

"You good, man?" I approach him, hoping it's not some message telling him his mom's gone.

He's staring at his phone, reading the screen like his life depends on it.

"What's up?" I step up next to him and read for myself since he's not saying anything.

Dad: Something's wrong with Mom. We're heading to the hospital. Get there as soon as you can.

My throat swells, making it hard to talk.

I finally manage to croak, "Do you want me to go with you?"

"N-No. Uh..." He swallows, slipping his phone away. "It's good. I'll just order an Uber and... and..." Pointing over his shoulder, he starts walking backward, then spins and breaks into a sprint, dodging bodies in the hallway.

I'm tempted to chase after him, but instead I pull out my phone and text Ethan's dad.

Me: Ethan's on his way. I hope everything is all right. Call me if you need me.

The message swooshes away, and I stay in the hallway until the "get your ass out of school" bell rings, telling us all to go home.

Unlocking my bike, I pull it out of the stand and get a message from Jack before heading off.

Jack: Thanks. Will keep you posted.

I slip my phone away, trying not to let the worry eat at me. I can't carry this shit home. My family has enough to deal with, and knowing how sick Ethan's mom is will only make mine cry. She's got a soft heart and feels everyone else's pain.

Cycling hard, I try to burn off some of my angst, dumping my bike in the garage before walking into the house.

I sense it as soon as the door shuts behind me.

The ominous silence makes my skin prickle, and I stop myself from calling out that I'm home. Creeping down the hallway, I follow the sound of running water and find Mama in the kitchen.

"Hola, Mama," I greet her softly.

She stops rinsing the dirty pot and glances over her shoulder. "Hola, mijo."

"Where are Sophia and Maria?"

"Uh…" Mama's voice is shaking, and she won't turn to face me. I let the bag slide off my shoulder, dread pooling in my stomach when it hits the floor and she flinches. "Maria is out with girlfriends, and Sophia is playing next door. I sent her right over as soon as she got home."

"Mama, estás bien?" My voice drops to a low whisper as I switch to Spanish. Since my dad's stupid white ass never bothered to learn his wife's language, it feels safer somehow.

She replies with a silent nod, and I know she's lying.

Walking across the kitchen, I reach her in three long strides, gently spinning her by the shoulders.

I spot the bruises before she can dip her chin, and my insides start to boil. "Where is he?"

"Sleeping. He needs to sleep."

"He needs to go to jail." I spit out the words, my Spanish sounding like a thick bark.

"Stop it!" she scolds, her eyes flashing as she looks up and tries to tell me off. "He gets those migraines. That's not his fault."

"He's got a migraine because he's hungover!" I point

to her swollen lip and the lump beneath her left eye. "That asshole doesn't have a right to hurt you!"

"He served this country. He fought for us, and it changed him. Are we just supposed to throw him out?"

I step back, gaping at her like I always do. "Yes, Mama. You throw him out. I don't give a shit if he has PTSD. Not when he refuses to do anything about it. Not when it means you turn black and blue. He's hurting you, and you're letting him. He needs help! He needs to go away and get help!"

"Don't yell at me!" she screams, then jolts and looks toward the staircase.

Her fear is so stark and painful. I know what she's thinking. What she'll never be willing to say. *Don't wake the beast.*

I let out a huff and lower my voice. "You can't keep letting him do this to you."

"I won't punish him. Not after everything he's been through. He deserves our respect. Our loyalty. If I can't keep loving him, who will?"

My face bunches as I make a fist, desperation rocketing through me. "He can't keep hurting you like this. What if he takes it too far one day? You don't deserve this, Mama."

She opens her mouth to respond, but all that comes out is a soft puff of air.

"No one will judge you if you make him leave," I whisper.

"And how am I supposed to do that?" Her expression crumples. "He needs me."

"No. He needs professional help." I swallow, leaning against the counter and having to look away from Mama's messed-up face. It kills me every fucking time. "I want to protect you from him. But you won't let me."

"I need you to keep your sisters safe."

My insides roil, my voice rising as a fresh wave of anger courses through me. "Even the fact that you have to say that is bullshit. Can't you hear how messed-up that is? This is our home. It's supposed to be a place of safety."

"Stop," Mom squeaks. "Please. I'm doing the best I can."

"I don't want him touching you again." I grip the counter behind me, my jaw clenching when she looks up at me and I get the full brunt of Dad's abuse. "If I'm here next time he goes off, don't expect me to just hide away."

"No. Liam. No."

"I'm bigger now." I stand tall, puffing out my chest and lifting my chin. "He might be stronger than me, but I'm not letting him touch you again."

She covers her mouth with her hand and starts to weep in earnest. Part of me wants to storm from the kitchen. Part of me wants to comfort her.

How is it possible to feel so much rage and sympathy at the same time?

Clenching my jaw so hard my teeth start to hurt, I wrap my arm around Mama's shoulders and give her a quick hug before kissing her cheek and walking out of the room. I can't look at those bruises anymore.

Shit, I want to go into Dad's room and pound his flesh while he's sleeping. It's what he deserves.

But I can't bring myself to do it.

When I was little, he was the best dad ever. When he came home on leave, I couldn't get enough of hanging out with him.

Then one IED in Afghanistan four years ago changed everything. He lost most of the guys in his unit, and he brought home a bag full of demons he couldn't shake.

So now we have to live with them too.

My phone buzzes as I reach my bedroom. Shutting the door as softly as I can, I check the message, hoping it's an update from Ethan.

But it's from Emily.

Em: You had time to think yet? What's your decision?

I huff and glare at my phone. This is the last thing I need right now.

Letting her down sucks, but seriously... I can't do this. It's not right. At least I don't think it is.

Shit, though. I kind of get her reasoning. It does make sense.

But why'd she have to choose me?

Scraping my fingers through my hair, I cringe at my reflection in the mirror.

I guess I should probably take it as a compliment, but...

"Dammit," I mutter, chewing the inside of my cheek as I glance back at my phone.

I poise my thumbs over the screen and type three different replies before settling on...

Me: No. I don't want to ruin our friendship. Sorry. You'll have to find someone else.

CHAPTER 16

Once again I arrive at school in a foul mood.

Dad was at the table for breakfast, looking all morose and cut up. Every time he glanced at Mama's face, he winced, and then his eyes would fill with tears. It took everything in me not to say anything.

Everyone else was probably feeling the same way, because it was a damn quiet breakfast. Even chatterbox Sophia didn't say a word. I hate seeing her like that, all sad and nervous, so I offered to walk her to school, just so I could try cheering her up.

By the time we reached her gate, she was giggling at my "would you rather" game. Can't believe she chose shaving her head over wearing an orange dress to school. That girl cracks me up.

Once I waved her off, I had to haul ass to the high school. I made it just as the bell was ringing.

I'm now sweaty and annoyed and—
My phone buzzes.

Ethan: Staying with Mom today. Take notes for me?

And shit. Ethan's not here.
I sigh and send back the response he needs to read.

Me: All good, man. I've got you. Give your mom a hug from me. Tell her to hang tough.

I would offer to visit after school, but I don't want to take my black cloud into any hospitals. I feel kind of bad but manage to justify my decision as I head to my locker. I'll visit tomorrow, when she's had one more day to get better. No one likes company when they're super sick, right?

Spotting Emily in homeroom, I give her a little wave like I always do. Her glum smile makes my stomach sink, and I work my jaw to the side, wondering if me not wanting to ruin our friendship has in fact... ruined our friendship.

When I take a seat next to her, she swivels her body away to muscle in on Toni and Nichelle's conversation.

Fine. Ignore me. Whatever.

Rolling my eyes, I grit my teeth and figure I just have to get through this fucking day. I'll keep to myself and focus on class. Whatever it takes to be drama free.

I'm pretty set on that idea all the way through until

lunchtime, when I walk into the cafeteria and spot Emily flirting with Brady Madsen.

What the shit?

I stutter to a stop, my eyes narrowing at the way her hand lands on his chest, her head tipping back with laughter. He's eyeing her like a piece of marinating meat. That asshole. The guy has one sporting code. He plays the game "How many girls can I bang before graduation?" I have no idea what his number is, but I will slit my throat before Emily becomes one of them.

Leaving the lunch line, I veer around the tables and stop behind Emily, crossing my arms and glaring at Madsen.

"Hey, Carlisle." Brady's smirk is punchable.

I clench my fists and force a smile. "Hey. Mind if I borrow her for a minute?"

Taking Emily's arm, I don't even wait for a response before pulling her away from Madsen's table and charging into the corridor.

"Hey," she complains, trying to shake me off, but I don't release my hold until we're around the corner and out of sight.

"What the hell, Em?" I throw my arms wide. "Don't. Just fucking don't."

Her eyes spark, her expression turning haughty as she plays dumb. "What do you mean?"

"I know what you're doing. Don't you dare give your V-card to that asshole."

"Why not?" She shrugs. "Maybe he can show me a thing or two."

"Fuck that," I scoff. "What happened to trust? I thought that was the most important thing to you."

"It was," she snaps. "Until the guy I thought I *could* trust went and bailed on me."

"Emily," I grit out, shaking my head and looking down the corridor.

"What?"

"What is your obsession with this? Why do you have to have sex right now? Why can't you just wait?"

"I explained it all to you yesterday, and my points were valid and good." She grabs my chin, forcing me to face her. "My body is ready for this next step. I want to know what it feels like. I want to satisfy these urges."

I get that. I really do. But...

"Can't you just touch yourself or something?" My cheeks heat with the whispered question, but she doesn't seem fazed by it.

"It's not the same and you know it. I want to know what it feels like to have a... you know... dick inside me. I want to experience sex. Real, actual sex." She mouths the last word, leaning close as we have this whispered argument.

How is she not blushing?

I'm ready to crawl into a hole of pure humiliation, and she's talking about this stuff with the clinical efficiency of a doctor.

We go silent as a group of girls walks past us. They

glance our way, obviously curious, so I relax my stance and smile at one of them when I catch her eye. She grins back, and they disappear into the cafeteria.

As soon as the door swings shut, I'm hunching back over Emily and whisper-barking, "Fine. I get it. You want to have sex. But not with man-whore Madsen." I spit out his name like it tastes bad. "Please. Not with that guy. You're worth more than that. Don't lower yourself out of desperation. Come on, Em. Have some self-respect."

She closes her eyes, looking thoroughly reprimanded, and my stomach clenches. There goes that anger-sympathy feeling again. Dammit.

Gritting my teeth, I glance to my left, noticing a few students walking out of the cafeteria. They look our way —more curious glances, although these guys know we're best friends, so they're used to seeing us together.

They're just used to laughter and teasing, not whatever this intense shit is between us right now.

Looking back down at Emily, I watch her bite her lip, her gaze kind of sad as it brushes over mine.

Shit. I'm letting her down.

And if I don't want her losing it to Brady Madsen, do I really want her losing it to some other guy?

At least if it's me, I can protect her. Make it safe. I wouldn't be going into this for my own selfish reasons.

Clenching my jaw, I let out a long, slow breath and finally mutter, "You're not doing it with him. You're doing it with me."

As soon as my words register, her eyes light up like I've just told her Christmas is coming early. "Really?"

"Yeah."

"When?"

I shrug, my stomach bunching into a knot so tight I almost feel like puking.

"After school today? My parents don't get home until late on Wednesdays."

Her voice is so high and hopeful. I can't go changing my mind now.

I nod. "What time do you parents get home?"

"Around eight."

"And your brother?"

"He's at college. We'll have the place to ourselves." She wiggles her eyebrows, and my insides sizzle as I look at her lips, wondering what they taste like. They rise into a smile as she leans forward and plants a peck on my cheek. "Thanks, Liam. I really appreciate this."

My lips feel tight and stiff when I try to smile back, but she's too busy grinning and doing a little happy dance to even notice.

"You're the best." Her voice is melodic as she does a spin, then walks off in that boppy way of hers.

I study the sway of her hips and picture my hands on them. Am I going to see her naked this afternoon?

Holy shit.

An awkward laugh bursts out of me as a horny fire starts to burn within.

I'm going to have sex this afternoon.

Sex.

I can't deny a small burst of excitement, but it's riding on top of a wave of sheer terror.

It's hard to know whether to punch the air with a "Hot damn" or cover my face and groan, "What the hell have I just agreed to?"

CHAPTER 17

I let Mom know I'm gonna be late home, feigning studying in the library. She buys it and is nice enough to tell me that she's had a great day and Dad left for work a few hours ago. He's a truck driver now and thankfully is away for a few nights on a long-haul delivery across the country. I hope he gets delayed and has to stay away for a couple extra days.

Knowing he's out of state makes it easier to breathe, so I head to Emily's house feeling lighter than I did this morning... but still nervous as hell.

I'm gonna have sex.

And I may have choked the chicken on more than one occasion, but I don't know shit about touching an actual girl. I know where stuff's supposed to go—I sat through sex ed—but I'm guessing it's not that simple.

What if she doesn't like it?

What if I screw it up somehow?

I'm damn near terrified when I ring her doorbell and have to remind myself that I'm doing this to be a nice guy. To help her out.

Her feet thump on the stairs, and I hold my breath when she opens the door. Her smile is unusually shy as she rests her head against the wood.

"Hey."

"Hi." I raise my hand, shuffling from foot to foot as I wait for her to invite me in.

"Thanks for coming." She steps aside.

I nod, easing past her and into the house.

I've been here a bunch of times before, but suddenly it feels new and weird. The clock in the pristine living room ticks, the fridge in the redone kitchen hums, and I can barely hear them above the pounding in my chest.

"So... um..." Emily points up the stairs and I follow her, the fifth one creaking under my weight like it always does.

"Do you, uh... have condoms?" I wince, hating the question but knowing it's necessary.

"Yeah." She glances over her shoulder. "I stole some out of my brother's room. He had a stack in his desk drawer, and I doubt he'll notice if one's missing."

I nod, forcing out "Good," but it sounds more like a croak than a word.

Her door whines as she opens it, but it's the click of her lock turning that really makes me tense.

This is happening.

I drop my bag on the floor behind her desk and

slowly turn to face her. My T-shirt suddenly feels too tight, and I give it a little tug because I don't know what the hell else to do with my hands.

Emily's fidgeting with the ring on her pointer finger, and when our eyes meet, we both let out these awkward laughs that sound like birds squawking.

"Okay, this is weird," I finally mumble.

"I know." She winces. "Why don't we just... um... Let's kiss. We've both done that before, right? I mean, not with each other, but we've both made out with people, and that won't feel too foreign, right? So..." She flicks her hands. "C'mere."

I do as I'm told, inching toward her until we're right next to each other. She looks up at me, her smile kinda cute as she lets out another nervous giggle.

"Let's close our eyes."

Sounds good to me. I snap my lids shut as her hands thread around my neck and she pulls me down to kiss her.

It's nice.

Her lips are soft and supple, the pressure good. My hands glide around her waist and I get into it, pulling her close against me and even letting out a little moan when her tongue slides across my bottom lip.

I open my mouth, letting her in and smiling at the sensation of her tongue touching mine. An electric spark seems to fire between us, and we dive into the kiss with more intensity. Things get kind of sloppy as we lick and suck and explore each other's mouths.

My body starts to heat up, letting me know it's good to take things to the next level.

I usually ignore it, because the girls I've made out with aren't ready for this kind of thing, but Emily wants it, so I let go and am soon poking her with my rock-hard dick while I palm her ass.

"Oh wow." She pulls away, staring down at my tented pants. The tip of her tongue skims her bottom lip before her eyes dart to mine. "Let's take our clothes off."

"You sure?"

She nods, looking nervous as hell. Her fingers shake as she starts unbuttoning her shirt.

I spot the edge of her white bra and my mouth goes dry. For a second, I can't move. I just have to stare at her, drinking in her milky skin as she sheds her clothes. Nudging the jeans off her hips, she lets them drop down her legs, and I can't breathe.

She's got a great bod.

Glancing up at me, she pauses, her eyes going wide. "Why aren't you taking your clothes off?"

"Sorry. I just... you... you're hot, Em. You're really hot."

Her cheeks turn a pretty pink, her smile touching me right in the chest as she bites her bottom lip and undoes her bra. Slipping it off her shoulders, she pulls it away, and I'm gaping at two perfect nipples. I've never seen nipples before—not in real life, anyway—and my dick is so hard it's starting to hurt.

As her thumbs slide into the top of her underwear,

she pauses. "Come on. I don't want to be the only naked one in the room."

I let out a short laugh and grab the back of my T-shirt, pulling it over my head and dropping it on the floor. It lands in a crumpled heap next to hers, and I stare at it while I unbutton my pants and let them fall.

Her breath catches and I glance up, not minding the look in her eyes right now.

"You're hot, too, you know." She says it fast, like if she doesn't talk quickly, the words won't come out.

My lips hitch into a grin, and I reach for the top of my boxers. My hard dick is making them look ridiculous, but I still pause, catching her eye and murmuring, "Same time?"

"Yeah." She nods. "One. Two. Three."

We both pull our underwear off, and it's happening.

I'm standing in Emily's bedroom butt naked, staring down at this mound of curls between her legs before skimming my eyes up her body and staring at her nipples again.

She bites her lip, studying my dick like she's mesmerized, and then she steps toward me and whispers, "Can I touch it?"

CHAPTER 18

Words are impossible, so I just nod.

Her eyes light with a smile as her small fingers wrap around my shaft, and holy shit, it feels good. She's just standing there holding it, and it feels fucking fantastic. I can't help a choked noise of pleasure.

This makes her smile, then she starts to rub up and down, which makes me groan. I reach for her shoulder, gripping it like I need help to stay upright.

"That feel good?" she asks.

I groan again, rasping, "Yeah, yeah. Real good."

She pumps a little harder, and I start to worry that I might blow before I can even give her what she's wanting.

"Wait. Wait, wait." I grab her wrist, slowing her down. "I don't wanna... I mean..."

Thank God she gets what I'm saying.

With a little nod, she lets me go and opens her desk

drawer. Pulling out the condom packet, she waves it in the air, then points to her bed.

I walk over to it and take a seat on the edge while she struggles to open the wrapper. Her fingers are shaking again, and when she sits beside me, I steady her hands and make sure she's looking me in the eye when I ask, "Are you sure about this?"

"Yes." Her answer is quick but emphatic.

She wants this.

I can see it in her eyes.

"Okay." I rest my hand on her bare thigh.

Her lips part, her breath catching, and I can sense her excitement... so I inch my hand a little farther up her leg.

And a little farther.

Her legs part slightly, so I keep going until my pinky finger is touching the soft mound of hair between her legs.

Her shaky breath hits my shoulder, her body quivering before she kisses the top of my arm, then trails her lips up my skin until she reaches my neck. She nibbles and licks her way up to my chin, and as soon as I can, I reach for her mouth. We share a deep, lingering kiss, her warm tongue sending spikes of pleasure firing through my body.

It's impossible not to explore her curves as she leans into me, and I'm soon massaging her boobs, running my fingers over her hard nipples and giving them a very soft pinch. They feel new and wonderful and—

Jerking away from me, she gives me a determined

look before unwrapping the condom and pulling it out. We both stare at it, glancing once at each other before she rolls it onto my upright dick.

It feels kind of weird. I've never worn one before, but it seems to fit me okay.

Emily runs her finger down the slippery surface. "Does that feel okay? Does it fit?"

"Yeah, I think so." I nod. It's not cutting off circulation, so that's got to be a good sign, right?

"Okay." She moves on the bed, lying back against her pillows and parting her legs.

I settle on my knees in front of her, too embarrassed to ask if I can take a look down there and see where I'm going.

Instead, I whisper, "Can I, uh... touch you down there?"

"Oh, yeah. Sure." She gives me a stiff nod, and I reach between her legs, gently exploring the area.

She gasps a little, then gives me a smile, silently telling me it doesn't feel so bad. I brush the spot again and her breath catches. Rubbing the area a few more times, I enjoy watching her eyes bulge and her lips part with obvious pleasure before dipping my fingers a little lower and finding her hole.

Brushing the tip of my finger around the opening, I notice how wet and slippery it is. I dip my finger in a little way, and she moans like this feels good.

I pull in a breath and figure it's about time we do this thing. Leaning over her, I set myself up, feeling kind of awkward as I try to line up my dick with the right place. I'm not sure if I've got my angle quite right, but I give a little thrust and meet resistance.

She hisses. "Wait. Wait."

I pull back, reaching down to find the place I'm aiming for and making sure my tip is sitting inside the opening.

"And you're definitely sure?" I ask one more time, catching her eye.

"Just do it," she whispers.

I ease into her, and she jerks beneath me. "Is that okay?"

"Yeah." She nods, her eyes widening a bit. "You're just... kinda big."

My smile is tense as I brush my finger down the side of her face. "Do you want me to keep going?"

"Yes," she whispers. "Just go slow."

So I do. I nudge a little farther into this tight space. It feels so freaking amazing—warm and tight and wet. It's hard to go slow when instinct is telling me to thrust and pump, but I push as gently as I can while her fingers dig into my shoulders.

"Keep going," she urges, so I go a little harder, and then she lets out this cry that makes me jolt.

I jerk up to look down at her face, which is scrunched up like I just hurt her. "Are you okay?"

She bites her lips together and nods.

"Do you want me to get out?"

She shakes her head. "No," she pants, her fingers digging into my arms now. Her nails are leaving little indents, but I don't want to point that out. I'm too busy studying her face to check if she really means what she's saying. I'm this close to pulling out when she whispers, "Just give me a second."

I stay still. It's a battle. My hips are begging me to start pumping, but she's not ready.

Watching her face, I wait until the tension starts to ease and her eyes clear.

Her familiar gaze connects with mine, and I'm about to ask her what she wants when she talks before I can.

"Start moving. Back and forward. You know, like they do in the movies."

I do as she tells me, slow at first, then building up my tempo as things get wetter and slicker.

Em starts gasping and panting like it doesn't feel so bad. Those little noises she's making are hot as hell, and I can't help going a little faster. Her eyes are closed and she's gripping my arms again, her fingers digging in as I build up even more momentum.

My body is buzzing, this feeling inside me starting to build. It's like I'm on the verge of exploding when she asks me, "Are you coming?"

"Yeah. I'm close."

"Tell me when." Her hands move to my shoulders, her breathing getting faster, like her body is building with something too.

I pump a little harder, and that intensity starts to

sizzle through my body, getting bigger and larger, expanding as if my body can't contain it anymore.

"I'm coming," I rasp in her ear while my hips jerk and I thrust into her again, a sensation rippling through me that feels so damn good that I think I might be blind and deaf. Talking. Not sure I'll ever be capable of that again either.

I fist the duvet beneath me and let out this choked sound, that can only be described as embarrassing, before my body finally starts to relax. This weight seems to stream back through my muscles as I struggle to catch my breath.

Leaning up on my elbows, I catch Emily's eye, and we share an awkward smile.

"Are you good?"

"Yeah." Her gaze dips to my shoulder. "I'm glad it was you."

"Me too." I brush my nose across her cheek but can't seem to look into her eyes again.

I don't know why, but suddenly it feels weird.

Suddenly I want to get out of her body and out of this house.

We just had sex.

I did what she wanted me to, and it felt fucking fantastic, but now I'm lying naked with my best friend, and somehow I just know that... we've lost something.

"Can you, um... get out now?"

"Yeah, sure." I move off her, shock coursing through

me as I glance between her legs and know for certain that things will never, ever be the same between us again.

CHAPTER 19

Present day...

"It was awkward as fuck." I wince, rubbing my eyes as I remember the next part and then make the mistake of actually saying out loud, "And it only got worse."

"How?" Casey laughs.

I groan, tipping my head back. I've gone this far, so I may as well finish this horror story with the nightmare ending. "Well... when I was getting off her, I noticed this blood, and for a second, I thought she had her period, but she said she didn't. And then I started to freak out that I'd accidentally cut her."

Casey throws back his head with a barking laugh. "It's a dick, not a sword, dude."

"I know, but I didn't know what a hymen was, and she obviously didn't know either. She gaped at her duvet, then freaked out too. She ran into the bathroom and wouldn't come out again. I tried to ask her what I could do to help, but she told me to leave." I let out a sad sigh. "She never looked at me the same after that."

They're all snickering, and I glare at them around the table. "Shut up, you guys. It's not like any of you have popped a cherry before, have you?"

They go quiet, glancing between themselves and then shaking their heads. I called it. None of them have done it with a virgin.

Ethan gives me a sympathetic smile before slapping me with the back of his hand. "You did a nice thing for her, man."

"Not sure she'd agree with you." I hitch my shoulder. "A few months later, she got together with that guy. You know, the exchange student. They fell in love, and she ended up traveling to Italy to meet up with him after graduation."

"Oh yeah. Dario or something."

"That's the one." I nod. "She told me after they got together that she wished she'd saved her first time for him." I roll my eyes, shaking my head.

"Well, you did try to tell her." Asher gets up, walking into the kitchen. As he starts pulling snack foods out of the pantry, he calls over his shoulder, "I'm with Ethan. You did her a solid. She asked, and you delivered. I wouldn't feel bad about that, and I'm sure there are far worse V-card losses in the world."

"Although I'm never gonna let you live down the fact that you thought you had a sword dick." Casey laughs, catching the bag of chips Asher throws at him.

"I didn't think I had a sword dick," I try to argue, but the damage is done. They're never gonna let me forget this.

"Still can't believe you didn't tell me." Ethan shakes his head. "You know, when I think about it... things *were* kind of different between you two. I put it down to Mr. Italy, but you guys were putting on a show before that."

"Hell yeah we were. It was awkward from that point on. We tried to hide it from everyone, but things were never the same." I shake my head in time with Ethan's, biting back my next comment because I don't want to make this bunch of sex fiends feel judged.

But ever since my time with Emily, I haven't wanted sex to be this onetime thing.

I felt like Em and I turned sex into this cheap, physical act that could be done with anyone.

But the truth is, I don't want it to be that way.

Since then, I've slept with a couple girls. Both of them were girlfriends already, and it was a million times better doing it with someone who wants to snuggle afterward.

That might not make me sound manly enough, but I don't give a shit.

I want to make love to my woman. I want to be able to

look into her eyes when I'm inside her. I want to make her writhe and moan and come because she means the world to me. I want to hold her afterward, and if that means I'm not getting some every second night like these guys do, then so be it.

I'm holding out for the real deal.

And sure, those two girls who I thought were... they didn't pan out. But that doesn't mean I'm not going to find my person someday. And when I do, I'm gonna hold on to her with everything I've got.

And I'm going to make love to her in every way I can.

And there won't be one second of regret.

Liam's story is out now, and you'll get to see him meet someone who steals his heart... but can he convince this wounded woman to trust him with hers?

Click this link to get The Heart Stealer: www.katyarcher.com/the-heart-stealer

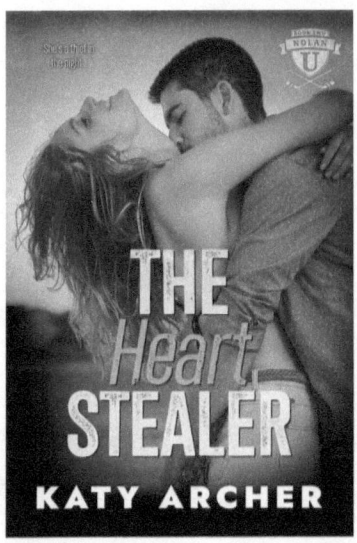

Once you've done that, you can keep reading to find out how Casey lost his V-card to the woman who gave him his first tattoo...

CASEY
THE MAN SLUT

CHAPTER 20

Sword dick.

Classic.

I'm never letting Liam forget that.

Sounds like a horror story for the guy, though. I guess I kinda feel a little sorry for him. But hey, he still got to have sex, and for me, that's a win. I fucking love sex. It's one of my favorite things to do, which is why I have so much of it.

Sure, they call me a man slut, but I seriously couldn't give two shits.

Sex makes me feel good.

I love women, and they love me.

I've never been *in love*, and I never intend to be. I'm not after something serious. With my family's DNA, that's basically impossible. There are zero committed relationships in the Pierce line. It's inevitable that I'll be flying my bachelor flag for eternity, but you won't hear me complaining about it.

Relationships—shit, even being friends with a girl—sounds way too complicated for me.

Give me a sweet puck bunny any day of the week. I love those chicks.

As far as I can remember, I've never slept with any of them more than once because variety is the spice of life.

I'm careful.

I'm clean.

I get myself regularly tested so I can keep riding the love train all the way to my grave.

Shit, what was her name?

My first time.

I'll never forget her.

She was small but strong, her muscles toned like granite. Her sexy little body covered in ink that was intricate. She was a walking piece of art. And her jet-black hair. It tickled my shoulders when we were first making out. I remember that.

And those brown eyes. They were pale brown—kinda coppery—and they mesmerized me from the moment she looked my way.

I can hear the shop bell ringing above my head and that catch in my breath when she turned and I saw her standing there.

"Hey." Asher nudges my foot with his. "Earth to Casey. Where'd you go, man?"

I snicker, my voice kind of dreamy as I admit, "Back to

Montrose. Summer of high school graduation. That chick. What the fuck was her name?"

"Oh, you mean Miss First Time?" Asher laughs.

"It wasn't *her* first time." I raise my eyebrows, making it abundantly clear that she knew exactly what she was doing.

"Nice." Ethan nods while Liam stares me down.

"What?" I raise my chin at him.

He rolls his eyes, tipping his head back with a groan. "Fine! Tell us about your amazing first time and how unforgettable it was for all the right reasons."

I crack up laughing and figure... why the fuck not?

CHAPTER 21

Three years earlier...

The cheers and applause from the graduation ceremony chase me home. It's fucking annoying. None of that shit was for me. I mean, I guess in a roundabout way it was, but when I took my diploma and shook Principal Carter's hand, no one in the audience was there because of me. I got the polite applause of strangers and the odd cheer from my teammates and the few girls who are crushing on me.

No one in that crowd was there just for me, though, and I hate that it's bugging me so damn much.

Walking through the trailer park, I kick an empty beer can across the loose gravel and watch it flip and turn, landing on the grass verge. The lawns need cutting, but I doubt that'll be done in a hurry. We don't exactly live in a high-end trailer park.

Our permanent trailer has been falling down around us since we moved in five years ago. But it's better than the one before that, so I'm not complaining.

Swinging the screen door back, I shove the door open. It's not locked. What's the fucking point? We've got nothing worth stealing in here.

Swiveling right, I head down to my bedroom, which has gotten smaller each year. I guess Mom didn't expect me to grow so damn big. She eyes me sometimes with this lost look on her face, and I wonder if I've taken after my father somehow. Maybe he was a big, bulky guy. He has to have been, because Mom's a small fry. She barely comes up to my shoulders now. I just grew straight past her sophomore year and turned from the chubby kid to a mountain of muscles.

Those are her words, not mine.

And again, I ain't complaining because this whole getting taller and stronger thing has opened a shit ton of doors for me. My hockey dreams have been (mostly) realized—shit, I can't even think about that right now—and girls now want to make out with me at parties.

Shrugging the shiny blue robe off, I dump it on the bed next to the graduation cap. The yellow tassel thingy dangles over the edge. I watch it swing for a second, trying to ward off this growing sense of unease.

Quick footsteps outside distract me, and I tense when the door swings open and Mom calls out, "Casey?"

I grit my teeth, tempted to ignore her, but of course automatically yell, "Yeah, I'm here."

She rushes down to my room, sounding out of breath even though it's only like seven steps. "Where were you, baby? I went to the school and you'd already left."

My lips twitch as I shrug. "The ceremony finished. I didn't see you around, so I figured I'd come home."

She leans against the doorframe, her large bracelets clinking together as she gives me one of her glum smiles. "Sorry I missed it. I was trying so hard to leave on time, but my asshole boss wouldn't let me go." Her pale eyebrows wrinkle as she unzips her purse and grabs out a cigarette. Her stress-meter must be running high. Her fingers are shaking as she lights up and takes a deep inhale. "Shit, baby. I'm sorry. I really wanted to be there."

"Don't worry about it. Those things are always so boring anyway." Shoving my hands in my pockets, I lightly kick at the floor, struggling to look at her.

I swear she's getting skinnier. Her tight-fitting clothes make it easy to spot. She's always looking so ragged, her curly blonde hair hanging limp around her bony shoulders. I swear her muscles look like they're shrinking.

But it's not like she eats a whole lot, and I'm pretty sure she's allergic to exercise, although she's constantly rushing around doing shit, like she's got this energy she just can't burn off.

I'm more likely to see a cigarette in her mouth than actual food. I'm sure that doesn't help with the weight thing either. But I'm not her parent. I can't tell her to take better care of herself. She'd just roll her eyes and tell me to mind my business.

"Let me see it." She snaps her fingers, holding out her hand.

With a soft sigh, I grab my diploma off the bed and pass it to her.

A genuine smile lights her face, and it's hard not to be affected by it. My chest swells, and it only gets worse when she murmurs, "Proud of you, kid. You did good."

"Thanks, Mom."

"I always wanted to graduate from high school, you know?" She inhales deeply, then blows the smoke into my bedroom. I watch it puff out her nostrils as she grins at me. "I was so determined my baby would."

I nod, not sure what to say to that. I'm the reason she never graduated in the first place. She got pregnant with me at the beginning of her senior year. And it was a shitty pregnancy. She was so damn sick that she couldn't go to school for months, but she was determined to keep me. She ended up quitting school before I was born and deciding that motherhood was as good a career choice as any.

But living with her parents and her newborn baby... well, I don't know the full story, but it got to be too much. So she cut ties to branch out on her own, only to discover that solo parenting was an expensive gig, and life wasn't the walk in the park it'd always been before.

So here we are now. Just the two of us, living in this shitty trailer park while she works two jobs she hates.

"Let me get a pic." Pulling out her phone, she holds it up while I wait for the ash at the end of her cigarette to hit the floor.

I brush my hand through the air. "Naw, come on. We don't need one."

"Oh, stop it. Put your gown back on. Come on. I have to post this shit. I want everyone to know my boy graduated from high school." She says it like it's the world's biggest accomplishment.

Maybe to her it is.

So I put my gown back on and settle the cap on my head.

She takes way too many photos, laughing when I finally get bored and start making faces at her. It's nice to hear that sound. She doesn't laugh much anymore. I've spent most of my life trying to make her giggle. When I was a kid, it was my number one mission in life—Make Mom Smile. Extra points for giggles and premium points for belly laughs.

I lived for it.

Until I realized how hard it could be sometimes.

Now I take the wins when they come along and try not to care about the other stuff.

She taps away on her phone, posting pics of me. I don't complain. She's smiling, and I don't want to ruin it. Maybe my grandparents will see. Unless she's unfriended them again.

Slumping onto the side of my bed, I hold my sigh in

check, rubbing my eyes and feeling eight years old all of a sudden.

"Have you decided what you're gonna do yet?" Mom's voice is soft. She knows this is a sensitive topic and has only brought it up a couple times.

I wish she'd just drop it already.

Talking about shattered dreams sucks.

Clenching my jaw, I keep my eyes on the floor. "I can't go without that scholarship, so..."

Mom's whine is soft and sympathetic. "There are other choices, baby."

"None that I want," I mutter, relieved to hear the buzz of my phone. I check the screen and grin. "It's my boys. I'm gonna split."

"Okay." She steps back, giving me space to shed my robe before I walk past her.

I give her a quick kiss on the cheek before heading out the door.

She never asks me where I'm going or what time I'll be home. I've never had a curfew. My friends are always jealous of that, but I don't know. Maybe having a parent want you home by a certain time wouldn't be so bad.

Shoving my hands in my pockets, I walk to the edge of the trailer park, laughing when Garrett's Jeep comes racing around the corner. Dust flies up from the tires as he screeches to a stop in front of me.

"Ready to party, bro?"

"Hell yeah." I jump in the back with Toby and Jamal, letting out a whoop as we pull onto the road.

Tonight's gonna be lit.

It has to be.

I don't care what it takes. I'll make my crazy ass do whatever it needs to.

Because I'll do just about anything not to wallow over the fact that I missed out on a hockey scholarship to my dream college.

CHAPTER 22

The party is already thumping when we get there. The honeys are out to play, and I sidle up to one as soon as she catches my eye. She's biting her glossy lip and giving me this sexy look. I know she's up for it.

At least I hope she is.

It'd be a nice way to blow off steam, you know?

Losing my V-card the night of my graduation. Yeah, I like the sound of that.

Most people in this school probably think I lost it years ago, but I'd never take things all the way without a girl's permission, and so far... I've struck out.

They let me touch and play, but so far, none of my hookups have wanted to slide into home base. Except that one time. But the condom broke when she was putting it on me, and neither of us was willing to take the risk. She said I could just pull out, but no fucking way.

My mom got pregnant the first time she ever had sex.

She's never told me, but it might have been my father's first time, too, and like hell I was gonna repeat history.

You know, that could be one of the reasons I've always been so happy to not take it too far. Pregnant in high school. Shit no. What a nightmare. In fact, any accidental pregnancy is something I will avoid at all costs.

When I do finally start having sex, it'll be protection all the way. I'm not knocking up some chick, because I'd never leave a woman to fend for herself, and I'd never leave my kid in the dust. There's no way in hell I want to be a father, so I will triple-wrap my meat stick if I have to.

So far hand jobs and BJs have been keeping me satisfied.

But I'm antsy tonight. Maybe sex is just what I need.

Resting my hand on Fleur's hip, I move to the rhythm pumping out of the bass speakers. Her fine ass is smushing up against my junk, and I grind into her from behind. Glancing over her shoulder, she bites her bottom lip again and winks at me.

Oh yeah, it is so happening.

Spinning her around, I rest my hand on the back of her head and gently nudge her toward me. She comes willingly, wrapping her arms around my neck and pulling me close. She tastes like beer, her warm tongue thick with the flavor. I wonder how drunk she is.

"Wanna go somewhere?" Her breath tickles my ear, and I nod, picking her up and walking away from the dance floor.

Her legs wrap around my waist, and she giggles as hoots and hollers chase us down the hallway.

"You up for this?" I murmur against her lips as she tries to devour me.

"Yeah, I want it." Her tongue starts painting my neck, and I close my eyes with a groan, accidentally walking us into a wall.

"Oof." She giggles again while I mumble my apologies and head for the first open door I see.

It's a bedroom, and I use the hallway light to guide me to the bed. Dropping her onto the mattress, I laugh at her giggling, but the sound is cut short when I start to worry about how much she's had.

Flicking on the bedside lamp, I study her face. "Are you really good? You're not so drunk you don't know what you're doing, right?"

She tips her head back with a groan. "Casey!" she whines. "I know exactly what I'm doing, and I've wanted this ever since we made out at prom." She gives me an arched look. "Remember? We were supposed to meet up outside, and you bailed on me. I waited out there for ages."

"I didn't mean to bail on you." I wince, running back to close the door. "I had to help Toby out. The guy was gonna get busted by the principal, and I couldn't let that happen. I've already said sorry like fifty times."

She lifts her chin, her amber eyes bright and demanding. "Well, make it up to me now, then."

Unzipping her skintight jeans, she wiggles out of

them, kicking them off her ankles before spreading her legs. My eyes travel up those long limbs, settling on that mound of ginger hair covering her pussy.

Hot damn.

Not only was she going commando, but she is one bold chick.

I know exactly what she's asking for, and I fucking love how gutsy she is.

With a smirk, I drop to my knees, wriggling my hands under her ass and pulling her to the edge of the bed. Her lips twitch with amusement as I rest her feet on my shoulders, then nibble my way up from her knee to her center, lightly caressing her inner thigh with my tongue.

Her legs tremble, and I pause before touching her pussy. "You sure?"

"Yes," she rasps, and I can feel the anticipation radiating off her.

It's hard not to grin as I lightly brush her clit with my finger before leaning forward to kiss her.

My tongue works its magic—soft licks and nips that have her squirming. She moans, writhing on the bed while her muscles quiver. Sliding my fingers inside her, I enjoy her mewling pleasure. It increases to high-pitched gasps when I start to pump her, and then she grabs a fistful of my hair.

"Oh my g—" The word is lost, turning into a throaty groan as the orgasm rocks her.

Her back arches, her gasping moans becoming this

satisfied scream as her heels dig into my shoulders and she rides the wave.

It's fucking hot, and I'm hard as steel when she flops back to the mattress, shifting away from me and laughing like I've just made her night.

"Damn, you're good."

"Thanks." I lick my lips and stand, grinning down at her... then wondering why she's scrambling off the bed and grabbing her stuff. "Wait... are you...? Are we done?"

With a simpering smile, she hikes her pants back over her hips and does up the fly. "Yeah, we're done. You *owed* me, jackass. You made me wait out in the cold for nearly an hour on prom night."

I lift my hand in the air, not even bothering to complain about it. I did. And even though this feels kind of brutal, maybe it sums up my year so far.

It started with a rejection letter from Nolan U and went downhill from there.

"Thanks," I call after her as she waltzes out of the room and I'm left standing there with a hard-on and a foul mood.

"Fuck this," I mutter, stalking back into the main living area.

Walking into the kitchen, I grab myself a cup of beer and find my buddies standing out by the pool.

"You get some?" Darius gives me an eyebrow wiggle.

I snort. "I *gave* some. Does that count?"

"Aw, dude." Toby gives me a sympathetic slap on the

shoulder, then starts looking around like he's scouting out hotties to make up for it.

"Don't worry about it." I nudge him. "I've got my beer and my boys. I don't need nothin' else."

We all raise our Solo cups and give a little cheer before getting thoroughly wasted.

I have no idea what time it is when I finally stagger home.

The trailer is dark, so Mom's already in bed, but even as I drag my drunk ass inside, I'm conscious enough to realize that the place is empty.

"Mom?" I shuffle to her bedroom, pushing the door open and sensing how deserted it is without having to turn the light on.

Shit. I should probably try to find out where she is.

Pulling out my phone, I stumble back to my room but haven't even managed to pull up her number before I'm flopping onto my mattress and crash-landing on Planet Oblivion.

CHAPTER 23

The sun is a mean bitch this morning, finding the one crack between my curtains and laser-beaming me right in the face.

I groan and roll over, my head feeling like a fucking brick.

"Shit," I mutter, my desert mouth making weird sticky noises as I try to figure out why the hell I feel so gross.

Closing my eyes, I beg for some more sleep, but it's pointless. I lie their restless, my body failing to get comfortable as I twist and turn looking for the perfect position.

It never comes and after who the fucks knows, I finally I stagger my wasted ass to the bathroom and do the world's longest pee before seeking out coffee. While it brews, I down three glasses of water, then let out a burp that echoes through the small trailer.

"Mom?" I call out, scratching my mussed-up hair as I walk to her bedroom door.

It's open... and the room's still empty.

"Shit." I lean my head against the frame.

She never came home last night. I can just tell.

I don't know where she spent the night, but she probably went straight to work from whoever her latest hookup was.

She doesn't have a boyfriend right now—as far as I'm aware—so it'll just be a rando who better have treated her decent. I can't stand it when she cries. Breaks my heart every time.

As much as she harps on about how all men, except me, are total assholes, she can't help looking for love, like her radar is constantly set to "seek a partner" mode. My whole life, she's gone from one fling to one boyfriend to one hookup after another. She even had an affair once. Can't believe she stooped to becoming the other woman. She even knew about it the whole time. It was messed up, and I told her to cut that shit out. Breaking up a marriage. What the fuck?

She only dated the guy for like another two months after he left his wife. I felt sick every time he stepped into our space. I was only nine, but I was smart enough to know it was fucked-up.

Mom stopped dating for like three weeks after I bawled her out, but then she slipped into a string of one-night stands.

I liked that better than Mr. Married. What a twat.

Grabbing my phone, I send Mom a quick text.

Me: You all good?

Mom: Yeah, baby. Had a girls' night out, now I'm heading to work.

Girls' night, my ass. Why does she feel like she still needs to hide what she does from me? I huff but don't bother calling her on her bullshit.

Mom: How was your night?

I send her a thumbs-up, then drop my phone on the counter before pouring coffee into the biggest mug I can find.

I'm about halfway through it when my Insta-scrolling is interrupted by a phone call from my boss.

"Hey, bud. Just wondering if you're up for work today. I've just had to send Ryan home. The idiot came in sick."

I snicker and check my watch. Working is the last thing I feel like doing, but the cash would be nice.

"Yeah, sure. I'll see you soon."

"You're the best!"

Becker hangs up, and I can't help grinning down at my phone. The head of my construction crew is a good dude. He treats all of us like the sons he never had, and I secretly lap it up. Other than my hockey coach, he's the closest thing I've ever had to a father, and I'm pretty sure

I'd do anything for the guy, which is why I race to get changed and end up running to the building site.

It's only down the road, and the exercise helps clear out the last of my hangover.

By the time I'm lifting planks and nailing in drywall, I'm feeling half decent.

There's a friendly vibe on-site. Thanks to Becker, there's always a good energy, and I fall into a happy rhythm.

Well, almost happy.

I can't quite shake the thought that this might be my future.

It's not a bad life, just not my dream of playing professional hockey.

I wanted it so bad. I worked my ass off all of high school. Hockey was the only thing I ever excelled in, and when Coach told me to apply for a Nolan U scholarship, I did it. Even though I was nervous as hell, I put it together, spent hours second-guessing every word of my essay, getting my application triple-checked by my English teacher and guidance counselor.

When the college scout came to check out my game, I played like a demon, willing him to fall instantly in love with me.

And then that letter came.

January sixteenth.

It'd been the one I was waiting for. I ripped that envelope open with the biggest grin... and didn't even make it past the second line.

Dear Mr. Pierce,

Thank you for your application. We're sorry to inform you...

Mom fished it out of the trash and read it out loud to me, even though I yelled at her not to.

The thing was, they were interested, but I hadn't quite made the cut, and there was no offer of a scholarship. I needed a full ride in order to go to a school that expensive, and every spot had already been filled.

There was no room for trailer park Casey Pierce.

It was the most brutal blow I'd ever faced, and I don't know if I'm over it yet.

Smashing the nail into the wood, I smooth my hand over it, then crouch down to continue the next one. Ryder has the nail gun, so I'm having to do it the old-fashioned way until the other one gets fixed.

It's good for my muscles, I guess.

I'll pound those nails in until all of this negative energy is burned right out of me.

And I'll stop thinking about the fact that this is the only life I have to look forward to.

It can't be.

I won't let it.

CHAPTER 24

My headache's back by the time I finally get home. Not to mention the fact that my shoulder muscles are killing me.

But hey, I earned myself seven hours of cash thanks to working late, and now I can put my feet up and relax.

The trailer is once again empty when I get home.

Mom's been back, though. There's some mail on the counter, and the dishes are done. She must have swung by between jobs.

With a sniff, I head to the fridge, grabbing a cold beer and cracking open the can. I've guzzled half of it by the time I wander back past the counter.

And that's when I spot it.

My heart stops for a second.

I have to blink and then rub my eyes like I'm in some kind of comedy movie. All of my movements are so over the top, but holy shit! Is that a letter from Nolan U sitting on my kitchen counter?

With shaking hands, I reach for it.

Half of me wants to throw it in the trash and not even bother.

But curiosity soon wins out, and I rip the paper apart, wrestling to pull out the stack of pages inside.

My swallow is thick as I force myself to read the top paragraph.

Dear Mr. Pierce,

Congratulations! We are pleased to inform you that a space has opened up in our hockey program, and you have now been admitted to Nolan University for this year's fall semester. Because of the late nature of this acceptance, can you please contact Admissions at your earliest convenience to confirm that you will be attending.

We have enclosed a starter pack with this letter so you can familiarize yourself with the campus and the opportunities and facilities we offer. Feel free to reach out to us at any time, as we would like to make this transition as easy as possible for you.

We look forward to having you at our university this upcoming academic year, and Coach Bergeron looks forward to seeing what you can accomplish on the ice as well.

Sincerely,
Monique Devlin

Dean of Admissions

I still haven't started breathing properly yet, because unless there's another sheet of paper under this one...

Pulling the letter away, I let out a strangled gasp as I read the top words.

Dear Mr. Pierce,

This is to inform you that Nolan University has accepted your application for a scholarship for...

I don't bother reading the rest.

The letter drops from my shaking fingers as I punch my hands in the air and let out the loudest "Woo! Fuck yeah!" I've ever made, then start jumping around the kitchen like a crazy person.

CHAPTER 25

I try to call Mom and let her know, but she's not answering her phone. I settle for a text, then call Coach.

"What the hell are you doing calling me after graduation? Would you go be on vacation, please."

I laugh and can barely form my reply, finally stuttering, "I-I got in. I fucking got in."

"Watch your mouth, kid. And say that again."

"I. Got. In. I got into Nolan U! Full scholarship and everything!"

There's a long pause before I hear a soft laugh. "Music to my ears. Hot dang it, kid. You did it!"

"I know. It's a miracle."

"It's well deserved. They should have accepted you from the start."

I run a hand through my hair, staring down at the letters on the counter. "I have to call Admissions in the morning to confirm everything, but... I kind of can't believe it."

"I can. Now get the hell off the phone and go celebrate."

I laugh and bob my head, still buzzing with so much energy I can't stand still.

"'Kay. Night, Coach."

"Hey, Casey."

"Yeah?"

Another pause and then words that will ring in my head for the rest of eternity. "I'm proud of you, kid. You deserve every good thing."

"Thanks," I croak before saying goodbye and dropping my phone on the counter. Right next to my acceptance letter.

I grin, shaking my head as I reread it yet again.

I'm in.

Nolan U.

I'm gonna be a Cougar.

A Nolan U Cougar.

"Yes!" I roar, punching both arms in the air again before snatching my phone back up, needing to find someone to celebrate with.

After twenty minutes of:

Jam: Sorry, dude. Stuck with the olds.

Gary-rat: I've already left on vay-cay.

Tobs: I'm too wasted to do anything but sleep.

Juggernaut: I'm gaming and can't leave. Come join.

I give up.

I'm not in the mood to game.

I need to go out. Get wild.

I'm so fucking pumped right now.

Racing through a shower, I change into something from my unfolded laundry basket on the floor and grab my skateboard.

Heading for downtown, I figure I can skate through the nightlife and find something to entertain myself. Maybe I can use my fake ID and hit up a bar or two. Dance with some hotties, throw back a few shots, get loud and crazy.

With a grin, I slam the trailer door shut behind me, whooping again when I think about the fact that very soon, this shitty-ass trailer is not going to be my permanent home anymore. A dorm room on Nolan U's decked-out campus will be.

It's a dream come true.

And I'm still grinning like an idiot when I cruise down Main Street, dodging human traffic and trying to decide which bar I should hit up.

But then I spot something I haven't really thought about before.

Jumping off my board, I grab it up, resting it against my leg as I stare across the street at *Ink Me* tattoo parlor.

I've walked past that place so many times and never really thought about it. Well, maybe I have, but not seriously.

Now?

Well, what better way to celebrate this epic win than with a permanent reminder on my skin?

"Why the fuck not, Case? Just do it."

Checking the road for traffic, I drop my board back down and glide across the street, figuring this will be a night I'll never forget.

CHAPTER 26

A bell dings above me as I step into the parlor. I glance up and check out the old-school brass bell before sensing a curtain swishing behind the counter.

"We're closing, dude. No time for any new tats."

My breath catches, my throat going dry as I drink in the stunner before me. She's a petite Asian in leather and tattoos.

I'm talking skintight leather. She looks like a biker chick with this vest thing that's a size too small and zips down the front. Even her pants have a zip down the front, and not just a fly. That thing goes *all* the way around, and...

Holy fuck that's hot.

I study her toned body, most of it exposed. Most of it painted with designs that draw me in. Everything from a lotus flower to a unicorn. She's a walking collage, and I can't take my eyes off her.

The design around her neck is mesmerizing—symmetrical patterns working from the center of her throat and winding around her like vines. Her smooth canvas would have been perfect for any artist. My eyes rise up her slender neck until I hit her coppery gaze. She's done that eyeliner thing where it kind of goes off the end of her eyes and curls up—like an Egyptian goddess or something.

She stares me down with a strong look that makes me want to drop to my knees.

This mystique is all powerful, which is probably why I still can't find my voice.

Her delicate lips twitch at the corners as she gives me a slow scan from head to foot.

She likes what she sees, I can tell.

I'm suddenly grateful my sleeveless T-shirt was at the top of my clothes pile. My arms are on full display, and I know they're looking ripped.

I can't help flexing them just a little.

She snickers and shakes her head. "Seriously. I'm about to lock up."

"Aw, come on. Please." I step up to the counter, words suddenly tumbling out in this incoherent waterfall as I rush to explain how epic this night is.

She tips her head, her eyes narrowing as she obviously tries to keep up with me.

When I finally pause to catch my breath, she holds up her hand to stop me from opening my piehole again.

"So, you got the scholarship and now all your dreams are coming true."

"Yes." I grin, stoked she understood all of that.

"And you want a tattoo to commemorate."

"Uh-huh."

Crossing those artsy arms, she gives me a pointed look. "You eighteen?"

"Yes." That's not a lie, but I get the feeling she wouldn't check my ID anyway.

Pursing her lips, she moves out around the counter, brushing past me as she heads for the door. With a quick snap, she locks it, spins the sign to *CLOSED*, and draws the curtains.

"All right, then, hockey boy. Let's go." She flicks her hand, and I follow her like an eager puppy through to the back.

The space past the curtain is sterile and neat. There are three tattoo chairs lined up and shining.

"I've just finished cleaning everything, but since you've got so much to celebrate..." She winks at me, and I think I just fell in love.

Grabbing a stool, she wheels it over to the end chair and takes a seat.

I climb into the dentist-looking recliner and try to get comfortable. I feel like I'm about to undergo surgery, and a flutter of nerves sprints through me.

"What do you want?" Her leather pants make a soft squeak as she takes a seat and eyeballs me.

"Uh... I don't really know." I shrug.

She rolls her eyes. "Fine. *Where* do you want it?"

I wince. "Not sure about that either."

Her laughter is an unexpected surprise. I drink the sound in, loving the shape her mouth makes, the sparkle in those pale brown eyes.

"Okay, well, since you've put zero thought into this, let me walk you through what you should consider." Grabbing a permanent marker, she rolls it between her fingers. "One, it's forever, and if you change your mind, getting it removed hurts like shit. Two, you don't want to regret it. Three, it should be something meaningful to you. So, have a think about something that you know you'll always love no matter what."

"Hockey." I say it without thought. It's an automatic answer, because hockey has always been my first love.

"Okay." She grins. "Hockey. Let me have a look here." She pulls out her phone and starts scanning for... I'm not sure. Until she spins it around and starts showing me hockey tattoos.

"I think I want something simple," I murmur as she scrolls through the images. I lean forward, her citrus scent wafting up my nose as I draw closer to her. It's hard to think straight, and I end up going for the first image that grabs my eye. "How about something like that?"

I tap the picture with the two hockey sticks crossing and the puck underneath.

"Is that too generic?" I cringe.

She turns to look at me, her nose a mere inch from

mine. Her skin is smooth and my fingers tingle, desperate to touch her face or skim my thumb over her lips.

"How about I add your initials?"

"CP," I rasp, because talking normally is impossible when she's this close.

"Hmmm." She purses her lips. "I'll think of something."

I lean back in the seat, unable to take my eyes off her as she gets to work sketching up a design. Her hands move fast across the paper, and I can tell she's a natural artist just by the way she holds the pen.

Within ten minutes, she's showing me an image that I'm instantly in love with. The stylized hockey sticks are crossed with the puck underneath, and above them sits a simple lotus flower.

"So you'll never forget me." She smirks, and I have to resist the urge to tell her I couldn't forget her in a million years.

How cheesy would that be?

Instead, I swallow, nod, and smile. I have no idea how idiotic my grin looks, but it makes her softly laugh as she holds out her hand. "I think your forearm would be the perfect spot."

I place my arm in her open palm, and she sets the design over it so I can see.

I nod because she knows best, right?

After a cold disinfect of the area, she transfers the image onto my skin, and then comes the painful part.

"Just black, I'm assuming?"

"Yeah. Keep it simple." I clear my throat, trying to not act as nervous as I feel.

The second the needle hits my skin, I can't help a small flinch. She grips my wrist, holding me still while she gets to work, and I try to hide how much this stings.

I mean, it's not unbearable, but it's not exactly a walk in the park either.

"This is pretty special, you know. Your first tattoo." Her eyes smile at me, and I focus on her face, the way her lips form different sounds. "Once you get one, it's really hard not to get another. If I had any more space left on my body, I'd definitely get more."

"Oh yeah?" I grit my teeth. "What would you get?"

"I have this vision of a big Japanese dragon. I'd have it on my back with all of these colors and surrounded by lotus flowers and greenery. It'd be fierce and beautiful at the same time."

"Sounds amazing." I sniff, trying not to flinch as she hits a particularly sensitive spot.

"Yeah. I hope I get to paint someone with it one day." She shrugs. "But if not, it's an image I can carry in my mind."

"What image do you have on your back now?"

"Hmmm." Her eyes dart to mine, melting my insides with her siren gaze. "If you sit still for me, I just might show you."

And there goes breathing.

I'm pretty sure my heart just stopped for a second too.

Her musical laughter skitters over me again, and now I'm fighting disappointment. She was only joking.

Shit. Fell right into that one, didn't I?

Even so, I stay still and quiet for the rest of the session while she describes her Japanese dragon in more detail and I float on the sound of her voice. It drowns out the vibration of the tattoo gun. It dulls the pain, and before I know it, she's giving my tattoo a final wipe and sitting back with a satisfied smile.

"Looks good."

I sit forward, staring down at my arm. Little drops of blood are forming over the ink, and my skin is pretty red and tender, but I get the idea.

"I love it."

I love it because she gave it to me.

I love it because it represents us.

I'll never say that out loud, and I don't even know what made me think it, but yeah... I fucking love it.

"It's a good way to celebrate, right?" She grins, preparing some sterile gauze to put over the tattoo and rattling off a bunch of care instructions.

It's easy to take in, and I agree to buy this special cream that will help the area heal quickly.

And then that's it.

She's standing from her stool, and I'm trying to find an excuse to stick around.

"So... I sat still." I give her a boyish grin that I'm expecting her to laugh off, but then she goes and shocks the hell out of me.

"You did." With a gleam in her eyes, she turns her back to me, scooping up her black hair and tying it into a bun, then unzipping the front of her top. The leather falls off her shoulders, and I study the various tattoos covering her back. She's got a book with flying pages on her left shoulder, a motorbike leaving a trail of dust on a dirt road across the center of her back. A phoenix rises from the ashes of her lower back and soars up to her right shoulder. And just down from her neck is a swirl of patterns that somehow ties the mix of images together.

"I wish I'd held out and gotten one big design, but I started and then had to create around what I already had. That's why I've threaded the swirl among the other images, you know?"

"It's beautiful." And I mean it. The colors, the ink, the shape... her body. It's all beautiful. "Any tattoos on the front?"

Yes, I'm a cocky little shit, but I gotta ask, right? If her back's this pretty, then surely her front is a stunner.

Glancing over her shoulder, she narrows her eyes at me, then gives me an impish grin before turning around and exposing her front to me.

My mouth drops open.

Holy shit. She actually turned around. I was expecting her to murmur, "Fuck off," before pulling her shirt back on, but instead she lets it slip off her fingers. It lands on the floor—a soft slap of leather and metal on the concrete.

And now I'm trying to remember how to breathe.

There's not as much ink on her front. Just a quote I can't read across her collarbone and some more flowery stuff around her belly button. But my eyes are kind of owned by those two fun-bags that are just begging me to play with them. I swear her nipples are pointing right at me.

"I can think of other great ways to celebrate, too, you know?" My voice kind of breaks on the last word because I know I'm punching above my weight on this one. She's a sexy-ass woman, and I'm just graduating from high school. She looks like she knows what she's doing, and I'm still holding my V-card.

I'm used to teenage girls who look at me like I'm hot property. They giggle and flirt their way to my lips.

I can't imagine this Japanese goddess doing either of those things.

But then she moves forward like a sexy feline, resting her boot on the edge of my chair before hoisting herself over me.

My breath catches as she leans toward me, her lips nearly brushing mine as she whispers, "Oh yeah? Wanna show me?"

"Hell yeah, I do."

Her smile touches my lips, and I'm gone.

Sunk.

Never to return again.

This woman is owning me without even trying.

And I'm 100 percent happy to let her.

CHAPTER 27

She kisses deep, her tongue exploring every inch of mine before she pulls back with a hooded look.

"Wanna touch me?" She's kind of breathless, which is fitting considering my lungs feel like they're about to catch fire.

I ignore the sting in my forearm and reach for her boobs. They fit in my hands perfectly and I stroke them, exploring the shape thoroughly before sitting up and pulling a nipple into my mouth.

She moans like she's enjoying it, so I suck a little harder until she's gasping and mumbling, "Yes. Aw. Yes. Yes."

I give the other one a little attention while my dick grows long and hard, straining against my shorts for release. It'll have to wait, and it better not do anything too early because this is fucking awesome, and I want it to last.

As I'm working boob number two, I hear the roll of a zipper and pull back in time to watch her pants pop apart.

These leather wonders zip all the way around, and I laugh in pure delight as she easily exposes herself to me.

"Touch me more, hockey man. Let those fingers do the talking."

She doesn't have to ask me twice. Popping her nipple back in my mouth, I glide my fingers over her stomach and right between her slit. I enter her with two digits, and she sinks down onto them with a groan that makes my brain fuzzy.

She's making those sizzling hot sounds because of me.

"Now here." She takes my thumb, placing it over her clit, and I start rubbing circles. I've touched enough girls to know what to do.

Shit, maybe that's why they always come to me.

They know Casey will deliver without demanding anything in return.

Is this gonna be the same?

Am I just getting her off so she's satisfied and I'm left needing a cold shower?

It's nearly enough to make me pull back, but this is so fucking hot I don't even care. Just watching this hottie fall apart will be the best gift ever.

"Ooo. Yes." She starts riding my fingers, tipping her head back and groaning, thrusting her chest into my face.

I'm working her with everything I've got, just waiting for that moment where her body will spasm with pleasure.

I feel like she's close. She's—

"Wait." She pulls back, licking her bottom lip before grabbing my chin and planting a kiss on my mouth. "I want to come when you're inside me."

She wiggles her eyebrows, and I nearly blurt that I've never done that before.

But I don't want anything stopping this epic moment, so I keep my mouth shut and nearly crumple with relief when she pulls a condom from her back pocket.

Seriously? She just walks the world packing condoms?

Don't think about it. Just be grateful!

She pushes my hand out from inside her, then makes quick work of my shorts. I raise my hips to help her out, and my cock springs out like a happy soldier.

He's eager as shit, a small bead already forming on the tip.

"Very nice." She bites her lip, grinning as she rolls the condom over me.

It feels weird and awesome at the same time.

I try not to reveal the fact that this all feels new.

Rising over me, she grabs my dick and wiggles around until my tip is poised at her entrance.

Holy shit. This is happening.

Like for real.

It's finally happening.

The epic thought nearly makes me blow on the spot, but I cannot let that happen.

Keep it together, Casey, or I'm gonna end you.

CHAPTER 28

A hot, wet pussy sliding down over your cock has got to be the best fucking feeling in the world.

Seriously.

Nothing beats it.

This sound comes out of me that I've never made before, a guttural groan that I couldn't hold in if I tried.

"Oh yeah," she breathes over me, her soft laughter like tendrils of pleasure weaving through my senses.

She starts to ride me, and I swear stars are forming in my brain. New stars that have never been discovered before. Solar systems that are Casey-made. Constellations that will have names like Caseyopia and HercuPierce.

Fuck. This feels so good.

Her lithe body continues to pump me, picking up speed like a piston. I grab her hips, my fingers digging into the misplaced leather as I beg myself to last.

I never want this feeling to end, but the build continues to sweep through me.

It's rising, my pulse quickening, my heart getting ready to erupt.

And then she starts panting too. It's mixed with these little yelps of pleasure that only make the brewing volcano bubble that much stronger.

"Yes," she starts chanting. "Yes. Yes. Yes!"

Fisting my T-shirt, her body starts to shudder, then goes taut...

And then she bares down on me, her insides clenching my cock while she lets out a high-pitched wail that sets me off.

I groan and squeeze her ass, this explosion of pleasure touching every corner of my body as I finally hand my V-card over to this tattooed vixen.

With pleasure, I might add.

And *hand it over* really is an insufficient phrase. I throw it at her, offer it up on a silver platter, cast it in gold and mount it on her fucking wall.

Take it.

It's all yours.

I pull her down a little farther until I've been milked for all I'm worth, and then slowly the blood in my veins starts to thrum at a normal pace again. My heart decelerates, and my limbs get heavy.

Damn. It's so fucking good. This sensation is floaty and languid and—

"That was awesome." She pats my shoulder like I've done a good job.

"First time." I kind of laugh out the words, wondering why I'm saying them. My brain obviously hasn't come back online yet.

"Really?" She leans away from me, trying to act surprised, but something in her eyes tells me she knew.

I don't call her on it.

Let's leave the conversation dead and buried, shall we?

If I end up asking if it was good for her, I'm gonna regret it for the rest of my life.

Leaning over me, her tits brush my chest as she whispers. "I'm honored."

The words mean more to me than I can even understand. All I can do is squeeze her waist and thank her with a quiet smile.

She gets off me, throwing a box of tissues at me before grabbing her leather top and disappearing out the back. I clean up, wadding up the condom with a bunch of tissues and shaking my head in wonder.

So that's sex.

Damn. I like it!

Her boots clip over the concrete floor, alerting me to her return. I pull my shorts up and adjust myself before rising from the chair.

By some miracle, the bandage over my tat is still in place.

"You remember all of those care instructions I gave you?"

"Yep." I nod, wondering if this is it. If I'll ever see this walking, breathing wet dream again.

She crosses her arms, giving me a kind smile. "You know, I don't normally sleep with clients. In case you're wondering."

"I wasn't actually, but..." I touch my chest. "I'm honored."

She laughs, shaking her head before ending our night with a tender kiss. "Take care of yourself, hockey man. Enjoy making your dreams come true."

"I will," I croak. It's hard to step away from her, but I make myself do it, because I can sense she wants me to pay up and get going now.

I head for the curtain that leads out front and stop just before pulling it aside.

"Hey."

She glances up with a smile. "Yeah?"

"What's your name?"

CHAPTER 29

Present day...

"Akari." I snap my fingers. "Her name was Akari. Can't believe I forgot that. She was..." I shake my head, unable to put into words everything that woman made me feel.

I have no idea how old she was.

Probably just a few years older than me. That's what it felt like, anyway. She had a young face and body. I like to think she was in her early twenties.

And I have no idea what happened to her.

"Congratulations, slut. Well done." Ethan starts clapping and the others join in, laughing at me while I try and pull myself back into the present.

But I can't quite do it yet.

Rubbing my thumb over the lotus flower between the hockey sticks on my arm, I remember her with a clarity that's supernatural.

She'll always stay with me. Her face. Her body. Her laughter.

I couldn't stop thinking about her after that night, and I went back a week later to see her again. But she'd moved on. Like an angel, she'd come into my life for that one night, then disappeared again.

But I'd always carry her with me.

Just like I carried other girls.

I eye up the different tattoos on my arms, a cacophony of symbols that I keep adding.

I may never sleep with a girl twice, but the ones who leave an impression get an impression.

They get a symbol on my body so I'll never forget.

Brushing my thumb over the diamond, I remember the blue-eyed blonde from the night I won my first hockey game as a Nolan U Cougar. And then there's the palm leaf from that girl I did on the beach when Asher took me on his summer vay-cay last year. She was a sexy thing from Brazil. We didn't even speak the same language, but we made our own that night. I couldn't ever let myself for get her. Or Cynthia. I brush the line of dancing music notes curling around my wrist as I remember the music major who rode me backstage after a soul-moving performance at her show case. The first time around, I took her against the wall in a moment of hot, frenzied passion. It was some of the best sex I'd ever had. We even did it a second time on the couch, and I swear in that moment, I loved her. The voice of a fucking angel that one.

I guess it sounds kind of cheesy and romantic to mark my skin with memories of these women, but that's the way I roll.

I'll never fall in love for real.

I'll never have just one woman for the rest of my life.

But these chicks on my arms have taken a small piece of my heart, and by the time I die, I'm happy to be left with a nub if I get to have all of these memories.

Casey's story is out now, and yes, he's gonna get the surprise of his life when a fiery redhead finds a place in his heart, and not even a little tattoo will help him get over her.

Click this link to get The Game Changer: www.katyarcher.com/the-game-changer

Once you've done that, you can keep reading to find out how Asher lost his V-card to a woman who should have been completely off-limits...

ASHER

MR. COUGAR TOWN

ASH

CHAPTER 30

Damn. I wish my story could be half as cool as Casey's. Some hot Asian chick banging you in a tattoo chair? Seriously, who does that? It's fucking hot. The shit pornos are made out of, and of course Casey has to be the one with that story.

I don't doubt for a second that it's true.

Casey is just the kind of guy to pull that shit off like it's no big deal. He was born cool. He'll always be cool.

Me? I've got to fight for that status.

Not that I will ever admit this to anyone, but I do sometimes wonder if the only reason these guys hang out with me is because it's my uncle's house we're living in. If it wasn't for that, would I even be invited to sit at this table?

Shut the fuck up, man.

Stop thinking like a D-bag and be part of this crew!

The usual reprimands fly through my head, and I

shuffle in my seat, putting on the smirk I'm famous for and psyching myself up. Because they're gonna ask me next, right?

I mean, part of me doesn't want to tell.

But then if they don't ask me, I'll feel like total shit, so they better fucking ask, you know?

I mean, it was hot.

But... well, it was also a bit of a train wreck.

Not a train wreck. I'll never regret it. Not like Liam regrets his first time. It was just... unexpected and maybe shouldn't have happened.

Desiree's big brown eyes flash through my brain and I internally cringe, still wondering if I should have gone there. I was seventeen and she was... forty-four.

Fuck. The guys are gonna eat me alive when they find that out.

I could just make something up, pull in a few little pieces of the truth as I throw something together.

But when every eye in the room turns my way, I figure I have to lay out the facts, plain and simple.

Sure, it's different.

But it was legal and definitely consensual, so... you know... that has to count for something. Right?

And you know what?

If I hadn't gotten a little frisky with "Aunt" Desiree, then we wouldn't even be living in this lush place.

So I have to sell this shit proud.

I did us all a great big favor.

And that's why when Ethan raises his eyebrows at me,

I lean back in my seat with a smug grin that quickly grows across my face. "You really want to know?"

"You know we do." Casey rolls his eyes. "Just spill, rich boy. Tell us how you stole some prissy academy girl's innocence on prom night."

"No way." I laugh. "Nothing that cliché."

"Oh yeah?" Ethan tips his beer bottle at me. "Come on, then, Mr. Original. How'd you lose it?"

I let out a nervous chuckle, rub the end of my chin, and think...

Fuck it. Here we go.

CHAPTER 31

Four years earlier...

I stand at the living room window, staring down at Central Park. It's one of my favorite views of Manhattan. I'm on the twenty-first floor, and the world below me looks small and white. Snow covers the ground, sparkling and pretty. It makes me feel like a king in my tower, looking over the landscape below.

It's so beautiful from up here.

Down below, it's all noise and bustle. The snow will turn to brown mush on the sidewalks, street dirt and traffic making the magical substance nothing more than annoying sludge and lethal ice.

Resting my forehead against the glass, I soak in the sight while I can. I'm home from school for three weeks, and the view here tops the boring ol' fields of Carrington Academy in Connecticut. Thank God I don't play rugby or football. I stand in the boardinghouse window, staring out at those poor schmucks hitting the freezing cold ground, and always rejoice in the fact that Uncle Hayes introduced me to hockey when I was three. Yes, ice is cold, but I'm padded up in an arena and don't have to contend with rain, sleet, and snow. Plus, I'm usually skating so fast, I don't feel the cold anyway.

I took to skates like a duck to water, and I fell in love with the sport.

My parents never understood it.

Probably because Dad sucked at hockey and hates that I'm so like his wife's big brother. I guess I won't shut up about how great he is. Maybe that rubs my father the wrong way too.

Well, I don't give a shit.

Dad's always going on about how great the twins are. It's not like he's tried to hide the fact that he wishes I was more like my older brothers.

"Asher? Where are you, honey?" Mom clips through the house, her heels sounding like gunshots on the polished tiles.

"In here, Mom."

"Oh." She jerks to a stop, staring at me like there must be something wrong. "What are you doing?"

I shrug. "Just looking at the view."

"Why?" She shakes her head, frowning like I lost three marbles on the way home.

"Because it's pretty."

"And a total waste of time," she mutters. "Would you please do something useful instead of just standing there? It drives me crazy."

I clench my jaw, shoving my hands in my pockets and gritting out the words "What would you like me to do?"

"I don't know." She flicks her hands in the air. "You're on vacation. Read a book, watch a movie, go out somewhere."

"Or stand at the window enjoying the view?" I point my thumb over my shoulder while she lets out an exasperated groan and backs it up with a big eye roll.

"Why don't you go pack for Colorado? Or better yet, check your email and see if you've had any more acceptance letters come through. Has Yale responded yet?"

"Not the last time I checked." I flop onto the couch, grabbing my laptop off the coffee table.

"They'll be in touch soon." She wiggles her eyebrows. "And then you have a choice to make. It's exciting times, baby boy."

I give her a tight smile, slowly opening my laptop and clearing my messages.

I've already been accepted to Princeton and Harvard. I guess either one of them would do. I wish I could tell her that I don't really give a shit where I go.

They're wanting me to get a degree in business so I can follow in my family's footsteps, which is probably a good move for me, but it's not that exciting.

Princeton has an amazing hockey program, so I guess I'm leaning that way, but—

"Heard from Harvard yet?" Dad walks into the room, lightly tapping my shoulder as he breezes past the couch, loosening his tie as he approaches my mother.

"He heard from them yesterday, Austin. We already told you that." She tuts and lightly slaps his arm with a laugh. "You never listen."

He shakes his head, pulling the crystal top off the whiskey bottle and pouring himself a glass. "I do listen, but if I don't hear the answer I want, then I'll just keep asking."

"Oh really?" Mom spins, resting her hand on her hip. "And what answer are you hoping for?"

"I'd like to hear my son tell me that he's accepted Harvard and doesn't need to bother checking his email like you insist he keep doing. Harvard's the one, Anna. I still don't know why you pushed him to apply all over the place. Bensons go to Harvard. It's what we do. The boys went there. Asher will go there." He sips his whiskey and frowns at us both. "Why do we keep having this discussion? It's not even a discussion. It's Harvard."

"Aus-tin." Mom draws out his name, her gentle way of giving him the finger. "We talked about this. It's Asher's choice. He doesn't have to follow in the twins' footsteps if he doesn't want to."

I keep my mouth shut while my head is screaming on repeat, "Like hell I'm going to Harvard! I never wanted to go there. I just applied because Dad wouldn't shut up about it."

My email dings with a new message, and I check the screen while my parents continue their bickering match over the best college for their son. Even though said son is sitting right in front of them and can hear everything they're saying.

Scanning the email address, my heart does this little kick, and I scramble to open the email.

It's from Nolan University.

Holy shit.

Is this...?

My chest deflates.

It's just an acknowledgment that they have received my application and it's now under review.

Under review.

How long does that take?

And why do I care so much?

"You get another response, honey?" Mom walks around the couch, leaning over my shoulder and reading my screen. "Nolan University? Why are you hearing from them?"

I bite the edge of my lip before letting out a soft sigh. "Because I applied there too."

"What?" Mom jerks back, and I force myself to spin and face the volcano. "Why would you bother doing that?"

"Because it's a good school. Uncle Hayes played hockey there."

Dad can't stop his snort of disgust and gets a stink eye from both Mom and me. But then she's fighting a grin as she wags her finger at him. "Stop it. Be good. My brother has done very well for himself. You're in business with him, for crying out loud. His company is one of your most lucrative."

"I know. I know." Dad waves a hand through the air. "I'm just teasing."

Yeah, right.

But he must have some respect for his brother-in-law if he became a silent partner in his real estate empire. And Mom's right about it being lucrative. My Colorado family is loaded.

Dad takes a seat opposite me, crossing his legs. His polished shoe swings in the air as the ice cubes clink in his glass. "So, Nolan U, huh?"

"Oh, don't be absurd. He's not going there." Mom struts away from the couch while I call after her.

"What about the fact that it's my choice?"

"From Ivy League schools, not some hick university in Colorado."

"It's one of the top colleges in the country!" I call to her retreating back.

"Whatever, Ash. You're not moving halfway across the country to live in Nolan." She says the town name like it's a bug she's just squished with her stiletto.

Pursing my lips with a sigh, I stare back at my computer screen, the Nolan University logo beginning to blur.

This is horseshit.

They go on about how I'm my own person yet totally control every aspect of my life.

I can't even stare out a fucking window and enjoy the view.

They'd argue that I have choices.

But it's like telling a toddler they can have the blue or the red plate. Sure, it's a choice, but it's a minimal one.

We're talking about my future here. This isn't some plastic plate situation—this is my life.

And I should get full say on where the hell I go to college.

CHAPTER 32

Christmas in Colorado is the best.

We're staying for New Year's Eve, too, so that's even better.

Mom and Dad don't care for it, but families have to make compromises, right? So they do alternate years.

And this year, I lucked out. We hit the tarmac in Denver, and I'm the only guy in our private jet who's smiling like I'm happy to be here.

Because I fucking am.

Life in Colorado is so much more relaxed.

There's no toffee-nosed porter on the bottom floor of the apartment building calling me sir. There's no apartment building! There's minimal traffic. It's just country roads with stunning views and then this lush, huge property with a sprawling mansion.

My cousins Harvey and Halsey are already waiting for

me when I arrive, and I jump out of the car with a whoop, diving into our standard group hug.

I used to spend my summers here when I got to be "too much" for my delicate mother.

She'd ship me to Cherry Hills Village, and I'd be the happiest kid on the block. This exclusive neighborhood just outside Denver has everything I've ever wanted. I would have lived here full-time if they'd let me. Screw prep school in Connecticut. Screw apartments overlooking Central Park. I wanted this as my life.

And I got it, I guess. In snippets.

"Ash-man!" Harvey slaps my back. "Good to see you!"

"Yeah, bro." I hug my cousin, treating him like the brother I wish I'd always had.

I got stuck with Adam and Antony. The twins are eight years older than me, and we have never, ever hit it off. To them, I'm the annoying whiner who they didn't ask for.

To be honest, I think I was a whoopsie, but Mom always assures me she's grateful I came along.

You know, that's why she used to ship me off any chance she could get. Or leave me behind when I begged to do one more week in Colorado.

But it never bothered me. Uncle Hayes and Aunt Carla are the best. I love being here with their awesome kids. My cousins are two years apart, and I'm in between. It's perfect, really.

We're the three musketeers.

"Let's go get wasted in the pool house," Halsey whispers in my ear. "I've already stashed the supplies there."

I grin against her cheek, gripping her shoulder to let her know I'm in, before putting on my good boy smile for Aunt Carla.

"How's my boy doin'?" She reaches up on tiptoes to hug me, planting a loud kiss on my cheek before holding my face and grinning up at me.

"I'm good. Even better now that I'm here."

She gives me a knowing little wink before patting my cheek and turning her attention to my parents. "Annabeth, so good to see you, honey."

Mom gives her a polite smile and a stiff hug. It's always been that way. Mom likes people, she just struggles to show it. Honestly, I don't know how she and Uncle Hayes are related.

"Big man!" Uncle Hayes wraps a solid arm around my shoulders. "Did you get taller again? I thought you'd stopped growing."

"I have. You just keep getting shorter." I smirk at him while he tips his head back with an explosive laugh.

"Haven't lost your smart ass, I see." Halsey gives it a playful slap before snatching my wrist and pulling me away from the family reunion.

"What? You're not going to greet the twins?" I raise my eyebrows as we run around the corner of the house.

She cracks up laughing. "I don't even think they realize they're in Colorado yet."

I roll my eyes. "They were bitching and moaning

about country life on the plane. I don't even know why they come to these things. They're fucking twenty-five, yet they still do exactly what *Mommy* tells them to."

"I'm sticking with my robot theory." Harvey glances out over the sprawling backyard with its perfectly manicured lawn and shrubbery. It's coated with a dusting of white snow, but some of the greenery is still poking through. "They were grown in a lab and raised by scientists for the first few years of their lives. Your parents got them potty-trained and perfect."

I start laughing as we crunch through the icy white powder, past the lush pool and around the hot tub. I should probably be defending my brothers, but I never can around my cousins. I never want to.

Antony and Adam are robotic. They live for business and are boring as shit. At least when I get told off for being on my phone too much it's because I'm playing a game or flipping through social media. They're on their phones constantly, researching business shit and stocks and whatever other boring-as-hell things they can think of in their narrow-minded, robotic brains. Neither of them has a girlfriend yet either. It wouldn't shock me if they haven't even been laid.

"Here we go!" Halsey sings as she opens the pool house door and dances inside.

I flop onto the L-shaped couch, kicking my feet over the back of it while Harvey and Halsey unearth the stash. It started out a few years back with a bottle of vodka that they snuck out of the liquor cabinet. No one seemed to notice, so we did it again.

My theory is that Daliah, the housekeeper, is letting us get away with it and replacing bottles before we get caught, but who knows. Uncle Hayes is a pretty cool guy. He probably knows and is just turning a blind eye.

Harvey lays out the shot glasses while Halsey lets out a triumphant giggle and starts to pour.

And that's how the rest of the day goes. We drink vodka shots and talk about everything from my college acceptance letters to the girl Halsey's crushing on to the girl Harvey hooked up with in the girls' locker room.

"Are you serious?" I sit up. "You did her in the locker room?"

"College is awesome, man." Harvey's laughter is all triumph. "Just wait until you get there."

Harvey started Lennox College this fall. It's one of Nolan U's rival colleges, and it's been this big thing in the house that Harvey chose his mother's alma mater instead of his dad's. They keep teasing each other about it, and the banter between them cracks me up.

Harvey's loving LC and constantly raving about how great life is. With stories like the one he just told me, I can understand why.

"I can't believe you didn't get busted." I bulge my eyes at him.

"We were quiet."

"And probably really fast," Halsey teases with a giggle.

"Shut up." He throws a cushion at her, knocking the shot glass in her hand and spilling vodka all down her front.

She gasps while Harvey does this giggle that only surfaces when he's drunk, and of course she has to retaliate. Cushion number two goes flying... and then we're suddenly ten years old again, screaming and laughing as we engage in an epic war that turns the pool house into a total mess.

Yes, we get busted.

Yes, we get yelled at.

Yes, we aren't allowed dinner until we've cleaned it all up.

Snatching the bottle of vodka, which spilled across the coffee table, Aunt Carla gives us her arched look, her nostrils flaring before she shakes her head and marches out of the pool house fighting a grin.

She's all bark and no bite, that woman. And I adore her.

Like I do every time I'm here, I wish this place was mine. I wish my aunt and uncle were my mom and dad, and I wish these two laughing fools beside me were my siblings.

I wish for a lot of things.

But can I make any of them come true?

CHAPTER 33

Christmas arrives with its usual chaos. We're surrounded by too many gifts and too much food, and I feel like a lazy, rich asshole by the time the day is done.

But now the fun begins.

With all of the Christmas stuff out of the way, the three musketeers can wreak a little havoc as we count down to the epic New Year's Eve party the Carmichael family always throws together.

Harvey, Halsey, and I hit the ski fields and spend a day boarding, we head into Denver for a little city action, and then spend the rest of the time pranking Adam and Antony, who are so pissed off after only day two that they bail back to New York.

Yes, there was yelling.

Yes, my parents are super pissed with me.

Yes, it was totally worth it.

It may be immature, but seeing Antony covered in

green slim and then Adam landing on his ass after tripping over our booby trap in the snow was fucking hilarious.

We laughed our asses off.

You know, it really serves them right for always being on their phones. If they looked up once in a while, they would have seen both of our pranks coming.

I'm still snickering as I slip on the polished shoes Mom is making me wear for the New Year's Eve party. She hasn't spoken to me since Adam and Antony left... except to tell me what I have to wear tonight.

It's a good sign. It proves she's thawing out and will have forgiven me by the time I leave for boarding school. She never likes to leave things on a sour note.

Adjusting my black tie, I smooth it over my white shirt and check that I'm looking presentable. Bensons always have to sparkle, stand out, shine brighter than the rest. I guess that's why Mom always makes such a big deal about how we look.

My laptop dings with a new message, and my heart rate picks up.

Even though I know it won't be from Nolan U (it's the Christmas break), I still deflate when I see it's just some advertising from one of the companies I follow. Deleting the message without even reading it, I sigh and slap my laptop shut.

The fact that my parents have outright told me I can't go to Nolan U makes me want it even more now.

But it's not just that.

Nolan is in Colorado. It's only a few hours from this awesome house and this amazing family. It's only an hour from Lennox College. I could easily see Harvey on weekends. If I make the hockey team, he might even come to some of my games, and I could show up at his athletics meets. It'd be fucking epic.

Running a hand through my hair, I rearrange it until it's sitting just right and stare at my reflection in the mirror. I study my clean-shaven face, my defined bone structure—just like my mom's. People always say I took after her, whereas the twins are replicas of Dad.

I rub my cheek, then pinch my chin.

If I'm completely honest with myself, I want Nolan U.

But my parents will be pissed. Mom will give me her disappointed face. The one that makes her lips pout and her big eyes get all sad. The one that always makes me feel guilty. And then she'll probably tell me not to be ridiculous and there's no way I'm moving to Nolan. Shit, they might even refuse to pay if I don't choose an Ivy League school.

Would they really do that?

I'm not sure.

Shoving my hands in my pockets, I frown and shake my head.

Shit.

I'm really not sure.

CHAPTER 34

A knock on the door hustles me along.

"Stop checking yourself out and get your butt downstairs. It's party time, bro!"

I smile as Harvey's laughter fades down the stairs.

People are already arriving, and I can sense the buzz of energy as soon as I open my door. Trotting down the steps, I scan the already crowded entrance and spot fancy people in fancy clothes greeting my aunt and uncle. It's all smiles tonight.

I stop midway down the stairs and take in the view, hoping for a few young hotties. Maybe I could hook up with one of Halsey's friends tonight. She always invites a million.

Spotting a blonde with sweet curves, I pause and take her in before flicking to the brunette beside her.

But then a flash of black curls catches my eye, and I turn to see her sweeping into the room. Staying on the stairs, I watch this vision weaving her way through the crowd. She's older, but damn... she is super fine. I have no idea if she's twenty-five or thirty-five, you know? She's got this smooth, dark skin, and her curves are lus-ci-ous. She's wearing a fitted black dress that pushes her boobs together. My fingers start to tingle just thinking about touching them.

But then logic kicks my ass and reminds me that I'm a seventeen-year-old senior, and I'm probably staring at one of my aunt's friends or something. She's gotta be a MILF, and I start looking for her kids.

"Desiree?" Mom's voice captures my attention. She lets out this squeal, and then it happens.

Hottie MILF walks right up to my mom with a beaming smile and gives her a hug.

They squeeze tight like they haven't seen each other in years.

"It's so good to see you. What are you doing back in Colorado?" Mom's voice carries across the room, or maybe I'm just straining to hear her.

Desiree whispers something in Mom's ear, and I make my way down the rest of the stairs, weaving toward the women.

Why?

I don't know.

I'm just drawn there.

"Oh no, sweetie. I'm so sorry," Mom's saying, rubbing Desiree's arm with this sympathetic frown.

The woman shrugs, her glossy lips pulling into a

pout. "What can you do, right? When they don't want you anymore, there's just..." Her voice trails off into a sigh, and that's when Mom sees me.

"Asher. Come here, honey." She waves me forward and I step up, trying to look cool when I glance at this stunning woman. Seriously, she's a knockout. I've never been so attracted to an older woman before. "This is my friend from high school, Desiree."

"High school?" My eyebrows shoot up. "Were you guys in the same class?"

"Sure were." Mom grins.

I'm speechless for a second. That makes this woman forty-four.

Forty. Four.

She's not twenty-five. Not even thirty-five. She's my mother's age.

And yet I'm still standing here totally entranced by her smile.

Her bright brown eyes drink me in with amusement as she extends her hand. "Hi."

"This is my youngest, Asher." Mom starts rabbiting on about Adam and Antony, but Desiree and I are kind of locked in a moment.

Am I just imagining this?

She's shaking my hand, and these prickles of pleasure are firing up my arm.

Holy hell.

I'm getting horny over someone who could be my mother.

When I think about it like that, it's kind of twisted.

Sick even.

But she's not my mother... and she's so fucking hot.

"It's nice to meet you." Desiree finally lets me go, looking back to Mom, who is *still* talking about how amazing Adam and Antony are.

"And how about you?" Mom finally pauses. "Did you ever end up having kids?"

"Nope." Desiree's thick hair swishes around her shoulders as she shakes her head. "You know me. I always wanted my career more than anything."

"And you've had it, sweetheart. I've been keeping an eye on you." Mom laughs. "CEO at the age of twenty-eight. It's impressive. And now you own three companies... or is it four? You're building yourself an empire."

Desiree hitches her shoulder like it's no big deal.

But then Mom's eyes bulge. "He hasn't tried to go after them in the divorce, has he?"

This sad look sweeps over Desiree's face before she quickly recovers. Her glossy lips tremble just a little as she forces a smile. "I think he still feels so guilty that he's happy for me to keep most of it. He's being overly generous, and I'm taking advantage while I can. I'm sure once the sparkle wears off Miss Twenty-Two, he'll come to his senses, but by then everything will be signed and sealed."

"You go, girlfriend."

I make a face at Mom. Those words should not be coming out of her prissy white mouth.

Desiree softly snorts with laughter and shakes her

head. Sharing a quick look with me, it's like she can read my mind.

"Oh, there's Kevin and Belinda." Mom's eyes light with a smile. "Hayes invited everyone tonight. Do you want to come say hi?"

Desiree glances over her shoulder. "Actually, I might grab myself a drink first."

"Okay. Asher, go get this lovely lady a drink, will you, honey." Mom goes to move away, then stops, grabbing my lapel and looking up at me. "Best behavior tonight. You understand? Do not embarrass me. No pranks. No shenanigans with your cousins. Be"—she pokes my chest with her finger—"have."

"Yes, ma'am." I tip my head with my good-boy grin.

She rolls her eyes but is kind of smiling as she glides away from me.

And then I'm left alone with this gorgeous woman who is checking me out with a bemused grin.

I clear my throat, glancing around the room and trying not to be annoyed with my mother for treating me like an infant in front of Desiree.

"So, how about that drink?" The tip of her pink tongue pokes out between her lips, and I have to swallow before I can speak.

"Sure." I squeak the word. I fucking squeak it.

She laughs and follows me toward the bar.

There are two bartenders working tonight. Yep, that's right. This house is big enough to have a bar that fits not one but two bartenders.

When my uncle and aunt first saw this place, one of the features that sold the house to them was this vast, open living area—bar included. They'd actually come to check it out as a property to sell but ended up falling in love with it and buying it themselves.

The house is designed for functions like this. It opens up to the pool area outside, and even though the winter wind has got the doors closed up, it still feels spacious with the glass walls and high ceilings.

I pause at the bar, watching the bartender closest to me put on a show as he mixes cocktails for two pretty ladies just down from where we're standing. They laugh and cheer him on. I grin, wishing I was half that cool.

"So, what's your flavor?" Desiree leans against the bar, eyeing me up like I'm interesting.

"Uh..." Rubbing the back of my neck, I try to play it cool. "Vodka martini."

Her mouth pops open with another laugh as she lightly slaps my arm. "How old are you?"

I work my jaw to the side, wondering if I should lie, but the word "Seventeen" pops out before I can stop it.

"So, you can handle your liquor, Mr. Seventeen?" Her teasing smile makes me grin.

"I do my best."

"Well, then..." She taps the bar, raising her finger to grab the bartender's attention. She has CEO written all over her, this woman. And her power is fucking sexy. "Two vodka martinis on the rocks, please."

The bartender glances at me, his eyebrows wrinkling.

"Don't worry." She winks at him. "They're both for me."

He gives her a disbelieving smile but makes up the drinks. Nerves have me watching his every move instead of eyeing the woman beside me.

My heart is racing for reasons I can't even explain.

It's not like anything is going to happen with my mom's high school buddy.

We're just having a drink.

Once that's done, I'll no doubt meet up with my cousins... if I can find them.

Knowing Harvey, he's got some chick in the pool house while Halsey is flirting up a storm with that girl she can't seem to get enough of.

What was her name again? Sandrine or something.

"Thank you." Desiree takes the two drinks and moves away from the bar.

I follow her around the corner to a slightly secluded spot behind the pillar.

"To New Year's Eve." She hands me a glass, and we raise them together.

"To meeting new people." I smile as we clink our glasses together and take a sip.

She licks her lips and grins. "So, I'm guessing I won't be telling your mom about this?"

"She won't care." I shrug. And that's probably true. She doesn't mind me having the odd drink, just as long as I don't get wasted and do something that will embarrass her.

My eyes skim over Desiree's face as she takes another sip of her drink. Watching her lips kiss the edge of that glass makes me wonder what they taste like.

But I shouldn't be thinking that, right?

I have to *be-have* tonight, and I'm pretty sure making out with one of Mom's friends falls into the *humiliate your mother* category.

Too bad.

Because I kind of don't care that Desiree's forty-four.

Those lips look supple and shiny, and I wouldn't mind a sweet taste.

CHAPTER 35

The alcohol gives me a nice buzz. I'm not drunk, just a little relaxed and enjoying conversation with this engaging woman.

She's got a head for business and won't tolerate any bullshit. It's impressive.

I listen to how she started her own business, building it from the ground up. She wanted to support her friend, who was a talented writer, so she learned everything she could about the publishing business. She helped her friend soar up the charts and start making a sweet seven figures a year before going into business with another woman she'd met online. This creative had a flair for clothing design, and she helped her friend set up a chain of boutique stores around the state and eventually across America. She became CEO of the company, which led her to meet her tech-savvy husband who wanted to design apps that helped people shop smarter.

With over two decades of helping people get their dreams off the ground, she now owns shares in multiple companies, and I can only imagine what she must be worth.

She's the coolest person I've ever met.

And not only has she wowed me with everything she's achieved, but she also seems interested in me.

"And what are you going to study at college?"

"Business." I shrug.

She gives me an assessing look. "Business."

"Yeah."

"You don't seem too excited about that."

"Well..." I tip my head, then sigh. "I guess. I mean, when I listen to you talk about all you've done, it's exciting. That sounds cool, but... when I think about the fact that I'm just going to study so I can join the family empire? I don't know." I shrug again.

She looks genuinely confused for a second. "Who says you have to join the family empire?"

"Uh..." I blink.

She laughs. "Expectations are a real bitch, aren't they?"

"Yeah." I chuckle, but it's a soft, breathy sound. The glass in my hand spins back and forth as I stare at the dregs of my vodka and wonder what she thinks of me.

"You know, I always find that success comes when you're doing something that lights a fire inside you." Her brown gaze softens with a smile. "What do you love?"

"Hockey." It's the first word out of my mouth, so it must be true.

"Hockey." She grins, her eyes skimming me like she's trying to see the muscles beneath my suit.

I can't help a smug smile as I straighten my back a little.

"How long have you been playing?"

"Since I was three."

Her black eyebrows slowly rise. "You must be good."

"I hold my own on the ice."

"I bet you do." She runs her hand down my arm, giving my bicep a light squeeze and looking impressed. "So, you want to go pro, then?"

"I don't know if I'm good enough."

"I'm sure you can be if you put your mind to it." She leans closer, her voice dropping like she's about to share trade secrets. "You know, you can do *anything* if you put your mind to it." Her brown eyes spark. "Life is too short to settle. Chase your dreams. Live them." There's that sad look blanketing her expression again. "Don't waste a minute. Because before you know it..." She snaps her fingers. "It's gone."

I swallow.

She licks the edge of her mouth and is obviously forcing a bright tone. "So, I say figure out what you want the most and go for that."

"And how do you know what you want the most?"

We're staring at each other with this intensity that makes me wonder if our conversation is packed full of innuendo or if we're genuinely still talking about dream chasing.

"Whatever makes your heart feel like it's dancing in your chest, that's the thing you should be going for." She lightly taps my chest, and my mouth goes dry.

If eyes could talk, walk, and dance, they'd be stripping off her figure-hugging dress right now.

I wonder if she can see it.

Her head moves back a little, her lips twitching with the hint of a smile as she dips her chin.

And then her sparkly clutch starts buzzing. She tuts and opens it, pulling out her phone and checking the screen.

"I better take this," she rasps, spinning and clipping away from me.

I watch her hips sway, admiring what looks to be a very firm, round ass, before a hand lands on my shoulder. "Son?"

I spin, sure my face is on fire as I'm greeted by my father and then introduced to a myriad of his friends.

He's showing me off like I'm his little Ivy League pony.

"He'll be accepted to all three, of course, so he has a choice to make." Dad's voice is rich with pride. "I say Harvard. Don't you agree?"

The people around us start up a healthy debate about colleges while I tune out and start looking around me.

I catch movement on the stairs and notice Desiree

disappearing up them, the phone still pressed against her ear.

I wonder who she's talking to.

I wonder if I can sneak away and find her.

The rooms upstairs are always empty at a party like this.

I wonder what would happen if I stumbled across her all alone.

Maybe we could keep talking about chasing dreams. Or maybe she'd let me live one of my very own.

Because, damn, that woman makes my heart dance.

CHAPTER 36

It's been thirty minutes, and Desiree still hasn't returned to the party. I can't stop checking out the stairwell, and now I'm starting to worry about her.

What was that phone call about?

Is everything okay?

Shaking yet another hand, I shuffle on agitated feet while I go through the palaver of explaining how I'm hoping to study business next year and then have to laugh and pretend it doesn't bug the shit out of me that Dad is pushing Harvard so damn hard.

He keeps squeezing my shoulder while we're talking. I'm sure it looks friendly enough from the outside, but all I can feel is this silent demand—*You will go to Harvard, son. You will go whether you like it or not.*

Finally managing to shake him off, I use the excuse of needing the bathroom to slip away.

"Then I'm going to try and find Harvey," I call over my shoulder.

It's a lie. I have no intention of interrupting whatever my cousin's got going on in the pool house. I'm sure that's where he is. And I'm sure it involves at least one naked chick. With the stories the guy has been laying on me all week, it sounds as though college has turned him into a total sex fiend. Maybe he was in high school too. He's always been a handsy kind of guy. It's just the way he's wired.

I get it.

Not that I've had sex before, but when I do, I'm pretty sure I'm going to love it.

When I reach the top of the stairs, I glance over my shoulder to check where my family are. Mom is engaged in some energetic discussion with an important-looking dude in a tux while Uncle Hayes and Aunt Carla are laughing together over some obvious inside joke.

Good. Everyone's distracted and I can now find Desiree.

It doesn't take long. She's actually in my room. I don't think she knew it was my room. It's just one of the many guest rooms, but I see it as a sign of fate that she's sitting on my bed.

Sitting and sniffing.

Shit, is she crying?

The door clicks shut behind me and she jerks, looking over her shoulder, and that's when I see them.

Tears are running down her cheeks. She quickly

slashes them off her face, and I want to tell her she doesn't have to do that.

"Are you okay?" It's a stupid question. Of course she's not.

"Yeah." She clears her throat, grabbing some tissues out of the box on my nightstand. "Sorry, I just... yeah, I'm fine."

Clicking the lock on the door, I ensure her some privacy and shuffle over to the bed. I doubt she wants anyone walking in on her this way. And I bet she didn't even think to lock the door behind her when she first came in here.

"Not a great phone call, huh?"

She tuts, shaking her head and mopping up more tears. "Just a bickering match with my ex. He's obviously starting to get over his guilt."

I take a tentative seat beside her, trying to decide if I should touch her arm or do something to comfort her.

"Sorry, this isn't your problem." She sighs.

"No, that's okay." I keep my voice low and hopefully soothing. "You can talk about it. I don't mind listening."

She lets out a watery laugh, glancing at me with a dubious frown.

"It's true. I'm a good listener." At least I think I am.

With another soft sigh, her shoulders deflate. "He left me for a younger woman. We'd been together for nearly fifteen years. Fifteen!" She huffs. "I thought that counted for something, you know? But apparently I'm always so busy and obsessed with work that I'm a cold fish in the bedroom." She looks bewildered for a moment. "I didn't think I was. I quite enjoy sex, but... he says I don't. So, you know... really, it's all my fault." Her voice pitches while her hand slaps against her thigh. "My fault."

"It's not your fault."

She gives me a side-eye that tells me she doesn't believe me. "It's not like he ever did anything to make me feel special or wanted. We were just living life together. I didn't realize I had to do anything more than be myself."

"You don't. This is *not* your fault." My voice is emphatic as I angle my body to face her. "You didn't *make* him cheat on you. And I can't imagine for one second that you're a cold fish. You're gorgeous and sexy, and any guy would be lucky to have you. I'm in awe of how driven and motivated you are. Look at all you've accomplished. You're amazing, and your ex is an idiot to walk away from you. He's losing big-time, and he probably doesn't even know it yet."

She's gone still beside me, and I don't really notice until I stop speaking. It's then that I suddenly become aware of everything, like the way I'm resting my hand on her lower back. When did I do that?

Or the way her eyes are drinking me in.

And the fact that her chest is rising in short puffs like her heart is racing.

Just like my heart's racing.

"You're so nice," she whispers, her trembling lips rising into a smile. "You really think I'm sexy?"

"Oh yeah." I bulge my eyes at her. "You're... you take my breath away."

Is that cheesy?

Shit. That's the cheesiest line ever.

I can feel my face folding into a cringe. An apology is forming in my mouth, but then she touches my face. Her long fingers brush my cheek, threading around to the back of my neck, and then she's moving toward me.

Her breath kisses my mouth just before her lips do.

I was right, by the way. Her lips are luscious and supple. My body responds automatically to her touch, and I lightly grip her hip. Tipping my head, I change the angle of the kiss, and before I know it, I'm brushing the tip of my tongue against hers. She moans as if she likes it, and then her tongue is thrusting into my mouth.

I match her need, deepening the kiss and feeling my insides start to boil... in all the right ways.

This is hot.

This is so fucking hot.

CHAPTER 37

I groan, threading my fingers into her thick hair and cupping the back of her head. My dick has sprung to attention and is now pulsing with a thick beat of its own. It wants something it's never gotten to experience before. It's a burning need so strong I'm not sure I'll be able to contain it.

Desiree moves on the bed, these little, desperate puffs coming out of her as she slides the jacket off my shoulders and starts pulling my shirt out from the waistband.

Shit, are we really doing this?

Her lips start trailing kisses along my jawline and down my neck.

Looks like we are.

Hot damn!

This is the best day of my fucking life!

My fingers tremble just a little as I glide them down

her neck and reach for the straps of her dress. They slide off her shoulders easily, and she's not wearing a bra.

She's braless and I'm now shirtless, and who the fuck knows where my tie ended up. This is so hot. My brain can hardly contain it while my dick strains against my pants.

Pushing her dress down to her waist, I pull back to stare at her luscious boobs. They're huge and round, her dark nipples begging me to taste them. I check her face to make sure this is all still good, and she gives me a little nod before I reach forward and give her breasts a light squeeze, rubbing my thumbs over her puckered nipples.

She tips her head back with a moan, and I'm mesmerized by her beautiful body, locked still for a moment by what's happening right now.

"Kiss me," she whispers, placing her hand on the back of my head and pushing me toward her luscious tits.

I go like a puppy racing for a treat. Sucking her right nipple into my mouth, I lick and play while she pants and moans. Her fingers fist the back of my hair while I do a thorough exploration, and then her hands are scrambling for my pants.

The sound of my zipper opening is like waiting for your favorite song to start playing. She yanks my boxer briefs down and my dick springs free, the air kissing it briefly before she wraps her warm fingers around me.

I lose concentration for a second, groaning against her skin.

That feels so fucking good.

She pumps me a few times, and I let out this guttural sound that I swear I've never made before.

"Are you about to come?" she puffs.

"I don't want to yet, but..."

Her hand goes still on my dick, and she pulls back to look me in the eye. "Have you ever been with a woman before?"

I want to lie. I want to make up some story about how I'm the stud of my school, but instead I have to sigh and admit, "Not like this."

"So, you're a virgin?" She starts pulling her hand away, and I snatch her wrist before she lets me go completely.

"Please," I beg. "If I'm going to lose it to anyone, I want it to be you. You're so fucking hot, and I want you so bad. I've never been so intensely attracted to someone before. The second I saw you walking into the party, I wanted you. You're so super fine. You... please don't make us stop."

Her eyes drink me in, so deep and beautiful. I lean forward and kiss those lips because it might be my last chance before she comes to her senses and walks out the door.

But she kisses me back and murmurs against my mouth, "You want to be with me?"

"So bad. You're sexy as hell. So fucking sexy." I say the words between kisses and swallow the soft laughter that comes out of her.

And then it's like someone's spun a dial, because I

thought what we were doing before was intense, but it's just rocketed up a notch.

Scrambling back on the bed, she hikes her dress up over her hips, slipping off her panties and spreading her legs.

"Come on, then." Her eyebrow wiggle has me crawling across the mattress.

Anticipation builds in me like a firestorm as I rest my hands on her knees and stare down at that perfect oasis between her legs. I'm about to have sex.

She sits up, pulling my pants down even more, until they're bunched at my knees, before brushing her fingers over my dick.

Her feather-soft touch sends sparks flying through my body.

"Do I need a...?" I point down at my rigid cock.

"No. I'm on the pill and you've never done this before, right? I'm assuming you're clean."

My head bobs like it's on a loose hinge.

"No blowjobs or anything like that?"

I shake my head... and it's still on a loose hinge, swishing back and forth like I don't know how to control it.

Her eyes sparkle with heat. "Then trust me, it feels better without one."

Nestling back against the pillows, she spreads her legs a little wider and beckons me with her finger.

Holy fuck.

It's so damn sexy I practically lunge at her.

She laughs as I lean over her, scrambling to get my dick in the right place. I poke around, thrusting with my hips, my aim slightly off as I wrestle to find my target.

"One sec, big guy."

I go still, letting her guide me inside her.

She's so hot and wet. The second her soft core wraps around me, I'm practically undone. I sink into her, barely able to breathe as the sensations wrap around me. This is the best feeling in the world. I will never not want sex, ever.

Holy shit.

I pull back a little, my body's natural instinct, and thrust back inside her.

She moans as if she likes it, and that sets me off. Two thrusts in and the firestorm is exploding. Before I can stop myself, I'm jerking inside her, coming like the total newbie I am.

Shit, what was that? Like two seconds.

I groan, burying my head in the pillow, too embarrassed to even look at her.

"Hey." She rubs my shoulder. "It's okay."

"No it's not. That was pathetic."

She giggles in my ear. "It was your first time, and you still felt really good."

"For like two seconds." I pull back, wincing as I slide out of her and kneel between her legs.

Dipping my head, I can't even look at her. This is a disaster and so fucking humiliating.

"Hey." She grabs my wrist, giving it a little shake. "Who says we're done?"

I go still, frowning in confusion as I look at her face.

Her smile is playful and kind. "I don't know about you, but I'm not done yet." Licking her finger, she glides it down between her breasts, circling each one. "My girls here could use a little more entertaining, and there's a spot right down here—" She brushes between her legs, tipping her head back with a moan. "—that would love a little of your attention."

My eyes bulge, and I let her take my hand and guide me to exactly where she means. She shows me where she wants to be touched, and I start turning circles over her clit.

She lets out this breath that tells me she likes it and then rasps, "Now kiss the ladies, Ash. Suck my titties, please."

She's talking dirty. She's practically begging.

This amazing, powerhouse woman is begging.

It's the sexiest thing I've ever seen.

I do as she commands, sucking those nipples and drawing circles between her legs until she's letting out these lusty cries.

Her body arches beneath me, her large boobs jiggling, as an orgasm rocks through her. I keep touching her, doing what she tells me she likes until she completely comes apart with a scream that turns my dick to granite.

Flopping back to the bed with this husky laugh, she

covers her eyes and admits, "I haven't felt like that in a very long time. You are good." She sings the last word, and it makes me feel like a fucking king.

Then her eyes pop open and she stares at my cock.

It's standing to attention, ready to play.

"Oh thank God," she murmurs, her grin playful as she wiggles her eyebrows at me and then spins around, thrusting her ass into the air. "Time for round two."

CHAPTER 38

I rest my hands lightly on her bubble butt, smoothing them over those luscious curves, and freeze up for a second.

She wants me to take her from behind?

Glancing over her shoulder, she wiggles her very fine ass. "Come on."

"Uh... okay. You want me to..."

She giggles. "Yes I do. It feels so good this way. Trust me. It's one of my favorite positions."

I raise my eyebrows and rise a little higher, grabbing my dick and wanting to make sure I line this up correctly. She's so wet she's practically dripping, so it's easy to find the right hole.

Nudging my tip inside her, I let out a groan of anticipation before thrusting forward. It's like a hot knife through butter. I glide straight into her wet pussy and bury myself to the hilt.

"Oh, you feel so good." Her husky voice vibrates right through me, and I pull back a little and thrust again. "Go hard, baby. Deep and strong."

She doesn't have to tell me twice.

Gripping her hips, I pull back until I'm almost out and then thrust again, deep and strong like she wants me to.

Her lusty cry spurs me on and I do it again, finding a rhythm that's thick and heady.

She likes it. I can tell by her breathy panting and moans of pleasure, so I keep going, grabbing her ass and pumping into her like a piston.

I'm lasting longer this time—thank fuck—and I enjoy every sensation firing through my body.

Taking her this way is magic. She likes it, and I'm in heaven.

Her cries are my personal drug and I pump a little faster. This energy building inside me is cataclysmic, and the orgasm hits me like a bullet train.

"Ah!" I cry out, burying myself deep before pulling back with another quick thrust.

I start to fall apart, thrusting again, a quick jerk, then a deep plunge. Using her hips like an anchor, I hold on, releasing myself inside her with this strangled groan that sounds like a dying cat. But I'm not even embarrassed. It feels so fucking good I can't even think straight. There's no room in my head for an emotion like humiliation.

My body is humming as she rises to her knees, changing the angle as she leans back against my body.

I cup her breasts, kissing her neck and shoulders.

She reaches up and threads her fingers through my hair, resting her head back against my shoulder. "That was hot."

"So hot," I pant into her ear before nibbling her shimmering skin.

As my body starts to float back down to earth, she moves away from me, shuffling off the bed and disappearing into my en suite. I flop onto the pillows, my pants around my ankles, and stare up at the ceiling. My chest is still heaving, and my lips won't stop smiling.

I just had sex with... my mom's friend.

Okay, now it's sinking in.

It was hot.

It was sensational.

But it's not like I can go around bragging about it. If this gets out, my mother will end me.

Plus, I don't want to embarrass Desiree. I doubt my parents will be cool with what she's let happen in this room.

The bathroom door opens, and I swivel on the bed to watch her creep back to the side of the bed. She's dressed again, looking fresh and in control, like she hasn't just been on her knees screwing a high school senior.

Clearing her throat, she tucks her hair back behind her ear. "Uh... you want to get dressed?"

"Oh yeah." I scramble to pull my pants back on, then jump off the bed and find my shirt. My fingers are clumsy as I try to do the buttons, and she ends up stepping forward and taking over for me.

"So..." She licks her lips, and my dick twitches. "That was amazing, and I really needed it." She glances up at me, her gaze softening. "Thank you."

"You're welcome." I let out an awkward laugh. "Thank *you*."

She finishes my top button, then rests her hand on my chest. "That can never happen again. And no one can ever know."

I cover her hand with mine. "I know."

"Especially your mom." Her lips tremble as she pulls them into a smile. "I think she might kill me."

I can't help a soft laugh. "I think the news would kill her before she could get her hands on you, actually."

Desiree groans and covers her face.

"Hey, don't do that." I gently pull her hands away. "I wouldn't write this any other way. Except for maybe the two-second mishap at the beginning." I wince. "But... this was... epic. Sensational. *You* are sensational, and your ex is a total jackass." I rub my thumb over her wrist, my voice growing thick. "Any man would be lucky to have you."

Her smile is filled with gratitude as she rises on her toes and kisses me. It's a sweet, tender kiss, and when she steps back, her eyes are sparkling. "Whoever gets you in the end is one lucky lady. Do her a favor and don't let her go, okay? Cherish her." This deep sadness passes over her face before she recovers. Her smile returns, and she pats my chest again. "Thanks for reminding me that I'm beautiful and desirable. I really needed that."

And after one more kiss to my lips, she brushes past me and walks out the door.

I'm pretty sure she took a piece of my heart with her, too, but I don't mind so much. She can have it.

Because as much as I will never tell anyone what happened in this room, it'll stay with me forever.

CHAPTER 39

Present day...

I've relived that New Year's Eve party a hundred times in my head. And this is the first time I've ever told anyone about it. I often wonder how Desiree's doing. I see her sometimes, at the odd function, and on a good day, we'll share a secret smile, other times she can't even look at me.

I'm pretty sure she's got a guy in her life again. He's a sculptor or something. A silver fox with tanned skin and a hot bod. He owns an art studio in New Mexico.

This is all secondhand information from my mom, but I can't help soaking it in, picturing Desiree in this new phase of her life. I hope she's happy. I hope this guy appreciates her.

I still haven't found my *one* yet.

It's not like I'm actively looking. I like the casual hookup life of college. I'm not after some permanent girl just yet. But one day. One day I'll meet a woman who will set my heart dancing, and we'll have hot sex all the time.

I can't help a grin as I come back to the present and take in the three amused grins.

"You lost it in Cougar Town." Casey slaps my arm with a loud whoop. "You dawg!"

"Your mom's friend. Holy shit." Ethan's laughing now, pointing at me and throwing his head back. "Has she ever found out?"

"No," I say emphatically. "And she never will. Believe me."

"Do you still see her?" Liam asks.

"Occasionally."

"Is it awkward?"

I shake my head, but that's a lie. It'll always be a little awkward. We have this big secret between us, and we avoid it whenever we happen to be in the same room together. Thankfully it's not that often.

"Dude." Ethan's shaking his head.

"Hey, don't judge me, man. If it wasn't for her, we wouldn't be sitting here right now."

"I'm not judging." Ethan shuffles in his seat. "And what do you mean? What's she got to do with this place?"

"Well..." I start fighting a smile. "She was the one who told me to only do the stuff that makes my heart dance.

So, when I got my acceptance letter from Nolan U, I thought... *fuck it.* My parents didn't want me going here, but that was the only acceptance letter that made me feel buzzed about college, so at my mom's birthday party, I announced to the entire family—and Desiree was there, by the way—that I had picked Nolan U as my college."

The guys all start grinning.

"Uncle Hayes was stoked, my mom started firing thunderbolts at me, and my dad just sat there shaking his head with this resigned look on his face."

"They must have been pissed." Casey laughs.

"Yup. But they couldn't back out of paying for it or anything because I announced it in front of everyone, and then Desiree caught my eye and winked at me. I could tell she was really proud of my decision."

"Nice." Liam bobs his head, looking kinda proud of me too.

"And then she went and did it again the New Year's after I started here. Dorm life wasn't going so great for me. Do you remember Duncan the Douche?"

"Ugh," Liam and Ethan groan in unison.

"Did that guy ever shower?" Liam mumbles.

"No! And he trimmed his toenails with his teeth." I gag. "Seriously, he was like a walking garbage dump, and he was obsessed with *Star Wars*. And I'm not talking normal nerdom here. That stuff's cool. But he was like next-level, 'the force is fucking strong with this one,' you know what I'm saying? He spoke fluent Huttese."

Beer spurts out of Casey's mouth before he cracks up laughing. Liam jumps up to grab a cloth to wipe down the table.

"Anyway, I'm explaining this to my cousins and Desiree overhears, then convinces Uncle Hayes that I'm old enough and mature enough to handle looking after one of his properties for him. She manipulated the entire conversation, and by the time the clock struck midnight, I had myself a six-bedroom house to look after and fill up with people I actually like." I spread my arms wide, indicating the lush house we get to live in here.

The guys all raise their arms with a loud whoop. "Puck yeah!"

I join them, and we holler, "Puck yeah!" a few more times before Baxter shuffles in and tells us to keep it down.

We wave our hands in apology and all glance at each other. It wouldn't take much to invite him to join us, try and weasel a V-card confession out of him, but our goalie is an entity of his own. I don't think he speaks any elvish or Huttese, but the guy is kind of quirky and likes to keep to himself.

He'll be graduating at the end of this year, and I wonder who we'll invite in for our final year at Nolan U. Hopefully I'll find someone as cool as these guys. Riley is definitely on the table. I like that kid.

Glancing around at my current roommates, I share a quick look with Ethan. He's still kind of dark at me over the bet, but I can't go backing out of it. He shook. He lost.

Now he must pay the price. Going without girls for a month won't kill him, and I can have some fun hassling him in the meantime.

I just need to make sure I don't push too hard or he might hate me forever.

Although we rub each other the wrong way sometimes, I look up to the guy, and I don't want to lose him as a friend.

Grabbing my beer, I lean back in my seat and listen to the banter between Ethan and Casey, watching these guys and quietly hoping that once we leave this place, we'll stay in touch.

It'd be so easy to go our separate ways, but nights like this seem to bond us somehow. We know one another's V-card stories now. That kind of shit makes you closer. I'll never admit this to anyone, but I hope we have more nights like tonight.

Because I want to be bonded to these guys for life.

No matter where I end up, I always want to have moments like this where I sit around a table drinking beer and shooting the breeze with my bros.

Asher's world is going to get turned upside down by a woman he can't stand. She drives him crazy—in both good ways and bad. But one thing's for sure... she's going to make his heart dance, even when he doesn't want it to.

Get your copy of THE LOVE PENALTY here:
www.katyarcher.com/the-love-penalty

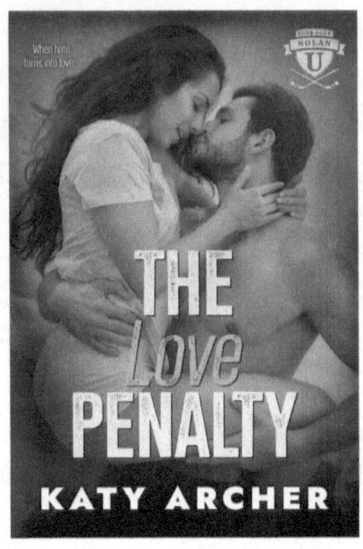

If you haven't signed up for Katy's newsletter yet, you can do that now. You'll get to download the Nolan U Sports Digest, which includes character interviews, plus a chat with Katy Archer herself.

You can follow this link to sign up:
https://dl.bookfunnel.com/zxddd7ow4c

And if you've enjoyed this prequel to the Nolan U Hockey series, please leave a review or star-rating. This helps to validate the book and let readers know it's worth a shot. I know there are a bunch of readers out there who love college sports romance as much as you do and it'd be great if you could help me reach them. Thanks for the assist!

DEAR READER...

Thanks so much for checking out this prequel novel. I hope you enjoyed getting to know the Hockey House guys a little more. I loved seeing how each of them lost their V-cards.

Losing your V-card is a big deal. For some it's wonderful, others awkward. It can be fun, romantic, embarrassing, meant to be, and the biggest mistake ever. Each person's experience is unique.

For some, they're lucky enough to lose their V-card to a true love or someone they really care about. For others, that's not the case. But whatever a person's experience, the coolest thing about sex is that it's a learning curve... and the more you learn, the better it can be. Practice makes perfect, right?

Also (and this is just my personal opinion), when you do it with the right person, it's mind-blowing. It's like a connecting of two souls, and it's fucking beautiful.

I'm so excited to see these four hockey house players—who think they have it all figured out—fall in love and have mind-blowing sex. I want to see them each connect with their person and know what it's like to make love and send the women who have stolen their hearts over the edge of ecstasy. I want their souls torn wide open and filled to overflowing by true love. It's going to be beautiful and amazing. And it all starts with Ethan—I mean Captain Hero.

Eeeepppp! I can't wait for you to read *The Forbidden Freshman*!

And just before I go, I'd like to thank a few key people:

1. My amazing team who are helping me with every step of this journey—Rachael, Kristin, Megan, Melissa, Maggie, Meredith, Trudi. You've all played really important roles in the creation of this series, and I'm so incredibly grateful for your help and advice.

2. You, my kick-ass reader. Thank you so much for taking a chance on this book. I hope you love the entire series.

3. The one inside me who gives me these stories, fuels my imagination, and has shown me the true meaning of never-ending, boundless love. Thank you.

xoxo
Katy

BOOKS BY KATY ARCHER

<u>NOLAN U HOCKEY</u>

Hockey House V-cards (prequel)

The Forbidden Freshman

The Heart Stealer

The Game Changer

The Love Penalty

...Also coming out in 2024...

The Only Goal

The Forever Game

<u>NOLAN U FOOTBALL</u>

Coming in 2025

<u>NOLAN U BASKETBALL</u>

Coming in 2026

CONTACT KATY

I love to hear from my readers, so feel free to email me anytime. You can also find out more on my website.

EMAIL: katy@katyarcher.com

WEBSITE: www.katyarcher.com

And if you want to connect with me on social and see pretty reels and teasers from the books, you can find me Addicted to College Sports Romance on...

INSTAGRAM: @addictedtocollegesportsromance

FACEBOOK: @collegesportsromancebooks

TIKTOK: @katyarcherauthor

xoxo Katy